# Healing the Billionaire's Heart

In the Name of Love
Book 2

Wynter Wilde

*To Kerrie,*

*Much love,*

*Wynter Wilde*

*x*

**For my family, friends and wonderful readers**

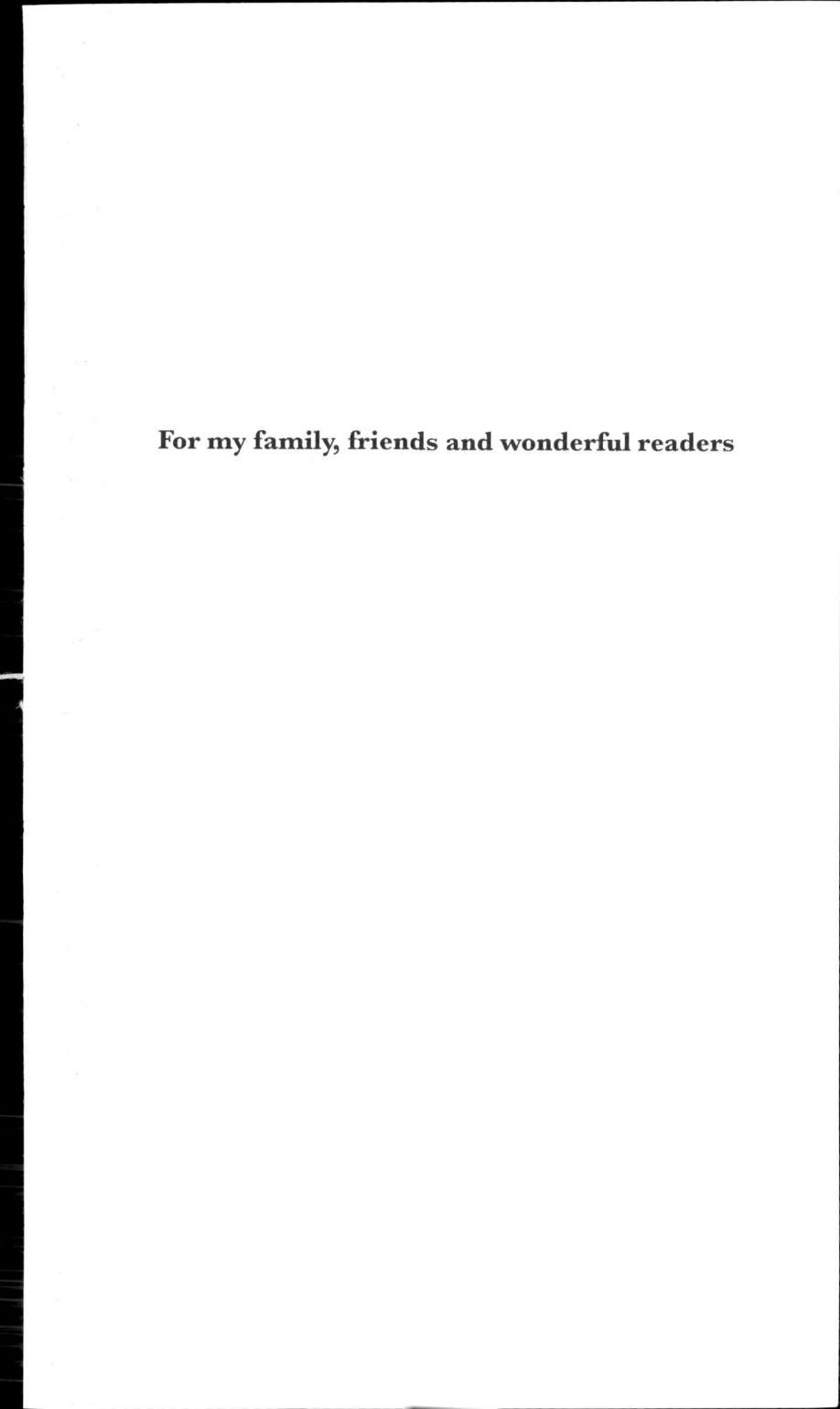

Copyright © 2024 by Wynter Wilde

All rights reserved.

No part of this book may be reproduced in any form or by any electronic or mechanical means, including information storage and retrieval systems, without written permission from the author, except for the use of brief quotations in a book review.

❧ Created with Vellum

# Healing the Billionaire's Heart

**Jack Kendrick:** These days, I guess I'm what they refer to as a sworn bachelor. Finding my teenage sweetheart in bed with my so-called best friend led me to rule out relationships. There's no way any woman is ever going to hurt me like that again. All I want to focus on is building my business empire and having a good time.

**Grace Cosgrove:** As wedding planner, you'd think I'd love weddings. I used to, until my mogul fiancé dumped me at the altar. Every wedding I plan breaks my heart a little bit more and I don't think I'll ever feel joy in my job or my non-existent romantic life again.

**Jack:** There's a wedding on the horizon and as best man, I have to get involved. I'm not overjoyed at the prospect but when I see the wedding planner... well... sparks fly in more ways than one. The groom tells me I'd better leave her alone, but I find her simply irresistible.

**Grace:** This could be the wedding of the year, a real-life Cinderella story, and they've chosen me to plan the wedding. It's brilliant for business, but it also means I have to summon some enthusiasm. Then I meet the best man and I wish he'd stop looking at me like that because I'm struggling to focus as it is.

*Will Grace heal Jack's heart, or will they go their separate ways before the wedding speeches are done?*

# Contents

1. Grace Cosgrove — 9
2. Jack Kendrick — 16
3. Grace — 20
4. Jack — 32
5. Grace — 37
6. Jack — 41
7. Grace — 44
8. Grace — 51
9. Jack — 58
10. Grace — 60
11. Jack — 68
12. Grace — 71
13. Jack — 76
14. Grace — 82
15. Jack — 86
16. Grace — 89
17. Jack — 95
18. Grace — 97
19. Grace — 102
20. Jack — 116
21. Grace — 121
22. Jack — 125
23. Grace — 129
24. Jack — 133
25. Grace — 135
26. Jack — 146
27. Grace — 152
28. Jack — 158
29. Grace — 163
30. Grace — 169
31. Jack — 174

| | |
|---|---|
| 32. Grace | 177 |
| 33. Jack | 180 |
| 34. Grace | 183 |
| 35. Grace | 187 |
| 36. Jack | 191 |
| 37. Grace | 195 |
| 38. Jack | 198 |
| 39. Grace | 200 |
| 40. Jack | 203 |
| 41. Grace | 205 |
| 42. Grace | 215 |
| 43. Jack | 219 |
| 44. Grace | 226 |
| Epilogue - Grace | 235 |
| Also by Wynter Wilde | 239 |
| About the Author | 241 |

# Chapter 1

## *Grace Cosgrove*

A hand lands on my shoulder, and I turn automatically.

'What ya doing?' My aunt Maisie Cosgrove smiles down at me.

'Planning.' I smile back. 'For the Cavendish wedding.'

'The handsome billionaire and his beautiful fiancée?'

'That's the couple. The real-life Cinderella story.'

Maisie places her hands on her chest and sighs. 'It's such a romantic story.'

'I know, right?' Ava Thorne told me all about it when I went to meet them recently. Edward Cavendish had lost his wife a few years earlier, so was dealing with his own demons. Ava was struggling financially, working all hours to support her mother and younger brother, but then she found employment as a nanny for Edward's son, Joe. While working for Edward, she fell in love with him and, as luck would have it, he fell madly in love with her. Now they're getting married and I'm their wedding planner.

My heart sinks a bit when I remember I should be ecstatic about landing such a fabulous job, but I'm just struggling to summon my old enthusiasm these days. It hasn't been the same for me since ... well, since the trajectory of my life changed in one fateful day and then the pandemic hit. Thankfully, that's in the rear-view mirror now, but it had a tremendous impact on me and my business, and it's taken me quite a while to get going again. Not that Ava and Edward will find out, of course, because I'll plan them an incredible wedding. Even if I'm working with limited time, their uncapped budget and the fact that their wedding venue is their home helps. And I've done this before, haven't I? Granted, I had to start back small and steady as a snail, but this is what I do. This is what I always wanted to do so I can and will get back on track.

'Do you want something to eat?' Maisie tucks her hands into the front pocket of her purple apron. At only five foot two, she's tiny, but I rarely notice because she has such a bubbly personality.

'I'm still full of breakfast.' I laugh.

'But that was hours ago.' She shakes her blonde head. 'You don't eat enough, Grace.'

My hands automatically gravitate to my rounded stomach and adjust my oversized black jumper. 'I eat plenty.'

'Coffee then?' She nudges me with her hip.

'Go on then but please make it black.'

When she's returned to the counter, I look back at my laptop screen, but the words there swim in front of my eyes. I'm tired today and have a bit of a headache because I didn't sleep well last night. The dreams I've had on and off for the past five years are back with a vengeance. I wake from them in a cold sweat, my heart thundering, and my cheeks wet with tears. The pain is sharp in the dreams; the fear is real, the humiliation raw. When I wake, it takes a while for the physical sensations to ebb away and for reality to comfort me. That last image makes me sigh because, for a while, reality was not comforting. Reality was bleak, lonely, painful. Reality was about cancelling plans, returning gifts and having to admit the worst thing possible. And then there was the crushing loneliness that I thought would split me in two because it was agonising. The long nights scrolling social media to find out things I should never have known. The seven stages of grief followed in migraine inducing technicolour: shock, denial, anger, bargaining, depression, testing and, finally, acceptance. I did the crime (by falling in love and trusting) and then I did the time (got my heart broken and had to get over him). One man almost destroyed me, but with time and patience, I learnt how resilient I am and that I can manage without him. I also learnt that I will never, ever trust another man with my heart. The only person I need is me. And my aunt and her partner. And my friends. But not romance. Oh no ... never romance! Ironic then that I am in the business of romance and planning weddings ...

'Here you go, sweetie.' My aunt places a mug of coffee in front of me, casts a glance around Cupcake Corner, the Notting Hill café that she owns and runs with her partner, then pulls out the chair opposite me and sits down. 'I can afford to rest my feet for five minutes before the lunchtime rush.'

Even though the cosy café has only eight tables, it does a roaring trade. Maisie and her partner, Riya, both quit their teaching jobs over a decade ago, sold their houses and bought the café, along with the flat above it that they live in. Where I also live, actually, and have lived for the past few years. I need to get myself organised and move out, give them some space, but it's hard with property prices being so extortionate and with the rental market so competitive. It's not like I haven't looked, of course I have, I'm a thirty-year-old business owner, but as soon as a decent property comes on the market to rent, it's snapped up by one of the hundred or so people who spend all day every day on Rightmove, Prime Location, or the other property sites. Some even pay estate agents to be the first to know about houses about to become available. Deals are made before I even find out about some properties, so now I find myself living in my paternal aunt's attic room (which is very nice), enjoying the delicious meals she prepares for me, and watching *Bridget Jones* movies and *Friends* episodes every evening for the millionth time. It's not a bad existence, but I know I can't stay this way indefinitely. I have a life to live and, as Riya says to me from time to time, I need to get back out there and make the most of being young. The problem is that often, after a day of work, I'm too exhausted to even think about much more than pouring a glass of wine, eating dinner and getting a good night's sleep. It was all going to be so different, but then someone stomped all over my heart and the life I thought I was going to have turned out not to be mine at all. This happened the year before the first lockdown, so you'd think I'd be over it by now. After all, it's five years ago, but something about the strange twilight zone effect of lockdown seemed to slow everything down and give it a sense of unreality, and it's only now that I finally feel like life is getting back to normal.

'Grace?'

I meet my aunt's dark green eyes and see the concern within them. 'Yes?'

'Are you OK?'

'Yes.' Nodding, I force a smile to my lips.

'You weren't just thinking about you-know-who?'

'Nope.'

'Really, love? Because you had that faraway look in your eyes that you get when you start reminiscing.'

'Doesn't reminiscing have pleasant connotations?' I chew at my bottom lip, then stop because I know I'll make it sore again if I keep worrying at it.

'Well, yes.' She rests her elbows on the small round table and leans forwards, holding my gaze.

'I was absolutely not reminiscing.'

'Were you thinking about cutting his balls off again then?' She cocks an eyebrow and I laugh.

'You got me!'

She leans back in her chair and nods. 'I've thought about chopping those brass balls of his off many a time for what he did to you, but I know that it wouldn't get us anywhere. Well, except for in prison but still ... the daydream helps when I see you sad and wish I could do something to make it better.'

I reach over the table and take her hands in both of mine. Her gold wedding band glints on the ring finger of her left hand and I rub it as if it can summon a genie to grant me three wishes. Her hands are small, the skin dry from endless washing, but they are hands that have held mine tight when I've cried, that have smoothed my hair back from my forehead when I've been feverish. They are hands that have made me endless meals and hot drinks, have run me bubble baths and helped make my bed when I could barely stand for the pain of my loss. She has worked hard to fill the void left by the loss of my mother to breast cancer when I was eighteen and my father in a tragic accident when I was just ten.

'You do make everything better, Maisie, just by being here. I'm so grateful to have you in my life.'

Her eyes shine instantly, and she closes them for a moment. When she opens them, a tear trickles down her left cheek and plops onto her arm. 'I am beyond grateful to have you in my life, Grace, and will always be here for you. I might not have children of my own that I carried in my womb and gave birth to, but I have you. To me, and to Riya, you are our daughter.'

I bring her hands to my lips and kiss them gently. My own emotion is choking me right now, so I don't even try to speak. When I release Maisie's hands, I reach for my coffee. It is strong and black and is exactly what I need.

Men will let you down, but loving aunts and strong coffee are two things you can rely on in this life. That's something I'm going to remember going forwards. I will never, ever, let anyone break my heart again.

## Chapter 2
## *Jack Kendrick*

The sound of running water wakes me, and I stretch and yawn. The Egyptian cotton sheets are cool and soft against my skin, and they smell like ... sex. Grey dawn light streams through the floor to ceiling windows of my central London apartment, but it's not raining outside, so why did I hear water?

Groaning, I sit up and grab my phone from the bedside table. It's just after five-thirty. My head aches and my mouth is bone dry. Too many glasses of champagne last night at a gallery opening in south London followed by hitting several clubs before heading home have left me quite hungover. And I'm not alone, it would seem. *Fuck's sake, Jack!* I stand and grab my boxers, then pull a T-shirt over my head and step into jersey lounge pants.

In the kitchen I make coffee using the fancy machine Edward got me for my birthday and open the fridge looking for breakfast inspiration. After deciding to stick with a protein shake, I make one up and sit at the kitchen island.

It's not long before I hear footsteps and I brace myself. What was her name again? *Cally? Sally? Lolly? Shit, I can't fucking remember.*

'Hey,' she says as she reaches the island and leans against it.

'Morning. Coffee?' I try not to look directly at her as if that can assuage some of the hangxiety rushing through me.

'Yes please.'

I slide off the stool and grab a mug from the cupboard, trying to remember if she told me she drinks it black. Deciding to chance it, I press the button on the machine, then place it in front of her.

'Thanks.' She perches on the stool next to me and I hold my breath. I don't remember too much of a conversation last night. I was more interested in what she was hiding beneath her red dress, although in all honesty, she wasn't leaving much to the imagination. Not that I make a habit of ogling every beautiful woman I see because some — those wearing wedding rings — are off limits, but she made it clear that she was interested in me, so I pursued her to see where it would go. That's the thing about me; I like the chase these days. It's the best part. It's fun, exciting, and sparks my interest — or my cock's interest — but when I've got what I want, I lose that interest in a flash. Fickle of me, some would say. I wasn't always this way, but that's another story for another time and right now, I need to get this woman out of here asap. I have work to do and the last thing I need is some woman getting all clingy and shit.

As she sips her coffee, I notice her shoulders are hunched forwards, her brown hair falling around her face. Last night, she had a sexy updo with tendrils caressing the nape of her neck. That got me going. There's something about a woman's neck that rouses something inside me.

'Everything OK?' I ask.

'Sure.' She turns on the stool, tugs the hem of her red dress down over her thighs, crosses her long legs and tugs the dress down again. 'Look, Jack, last night was fun but—'

'*Halle!*' Laughter spills out of me as I point at her.

She frowns. 'What?'

'Your name.'

'Of course that's my name. Did you forget?'

'No.' I swallow. 'It's just a ... a nice name.'

'Thanks.' She looks down at her coffee, then back up at me. 'Look, as I was saying, I need to get going. Last night was fun but no one needs to know about it do they?'

'What do you mean?'

'Well, see Jack, the thing is ... I-I'm married.'

'You're what?'

'I'm married. My husband works away, and I get lonely and then last night, you seemed so nice and ... well ... I was quite tipsy and ... the sex was pretty amazing and ... but ... I need to go.'

'You're fucking married?' My jaw clenches as I stand. 'I don't screw married women.'

It's against the rules. I don't want a relationship, but I don't want to hurt anyone either. She gave me no sign that she was married last night and if she had, I would most certainly have come home alone. 'I think you should go. *Now!*' The last word emerges as a bark and she flinches.

'I'm sorry, Jack. I didn't mean to deceive you I just ... got carried away. But please ... there's no need for anyone to know about this is there?' Her repetition of the question irritates me. If you don't like the heat, stay out of the kitchen.

'No one will hear anything from me.' I cross the kitchen and dump my mug and glass in the sink, then stand there for a moment, breathing deep as I try to calm down. *Married, for fuck's sake!*

'Jack.' Her hand on my shoulder. Her breath on my neck. Her sweet perfume cloying and turning my stomach. 'I'm sorry. I didn't mean to hurt you.'

I laugh and it sounds hard and cold. When I turn, I see confusion in her brown eyes. 'You could never hurt me, Halle. No one can ever hurt me. Can you see yourself out?'

Without waiting for an answer, I march to my bedroom and into the ensuite, then turn the shower on. When I step under the hot, powerful spray, I force all feelings from my mind, release them from my body, and scrub away the previous night's sex. All it was to me was sex. A physical act. Nothing more. After what I've been through, I'll never ask for more that, but only if a woman is single. Next time, I will definitely fucking check before I bring a woman home.

# Chapter 3

## *Grace*

'Champagne?' The young man holds out a tray with three flutes of bubbly at the centre. I hesitate, about to decline, but then change my mind.

'Thank you.' I accept a flute and take a sip, reminding myself not to drink it too quickly. After all, it's not even eleven, and I skipped breakfast this morning because I wanted to make sure I got here on time to meet Ava and her mum, Nancy. They are in the changing room and I am waiting in the plushly carpeted area outside, my laptop and iPhone on the seat next to me, my feet throbbing in my heels. I should have worn flats to walk here, but I wanted to look smart and now I'm regretting it. Londoners know to wear sensible shoes and bring heels for later.

*Focus on the champagne,* I tell myself, and take another sip. Perhaps it will numb my toes.

Music, either from a classical CD or a download, fills the room, while the air is laced with the fragrance of lilies. Probably because there are large vases of fresh flowers everywhere you look, creating that all-important wedding vibe to encourage customers to *spend spend spend*.

I suggested a list of wedding dress shops to Ava and Edward and this was the one she chose. It's not the most expensive one, not by a long shot, but it's not cheap either. Then again, it's difficult to pick up a cheap wedding dress these days, even off the rail. Ava said she's satisfied with a ready-made dress, but Edward suggested a trip to Paris for a bespoke gown. She declined that offer, saying shyly that it seemed frivolous, as well as his offer of a designer gown from one of his contacts. She wants as little fuss as possible, bless her, and it makes me like her even more.

Ava is young and sweet, naturally beautiful and very warm. Edward is handsome and rich and could have had his pick of eligible women, but he chose Ava because he loves her and I can see why. She doesn't seem to have an evil bone in her body, and the way she looks at him makes my heart squeeze. She clearly adores him and would do anything for him, yet there's a vulnerability about her that makes me worry for her. I hope he never hurts her. I'm sure he won't, though. He looks at her like she's the most incredible thing he's ever seen in his life and like he'd be lost without her. They love each other and I hope it lasts. I groan inwardly because I'm a wedding planner and I shouldn't be so damned cynical. I really need to get past this because it could affect my work, affect the success of my business and after having to put my life on pause, I need to get things going again, to prove to the world that I am good at what I do. Word of mouth is everything in this business, and I need Edward and Ava to sing my praises. This wedding could make or break me. I have planned several weddings since my world imploded, but they were more low key and I did them at a bargain price because I was trying to re-establish myself. But now, this wedding, this is the big one for me, my fresh start, and so it has to go well.

Nancy pops her head around the changing room door and I see that her light brown eyes are rimmed with red. Standing up, I place my champagne on a side table then ask, 'Everything all right?'

'She's just ... s-so beautiful.' Nancy opens the door a bit more and steps out, then closes it behind her. 'I knew this would be an emotional day, but I had no idea how much it would choke me up seeing my baby as a bride.'

'I can't wait to see the dress.' I rub Nancy's arm to offer her comfort and she smiles at me, then pushes a hand through her short brown hair.

'When he sees her on their wedding day, Edward will be completely besotted.'

The changing room door opens again, and my chest tightens. I've seen a lot of brides over the years, but I suddenly feel nervous about seeing Ava. Maybe it's because she's so sweet and because I want this to be perfect for her. Maybe it's because I'm softer than I want to be. But when I see her, my breath catches in my throat and my vision blurs.

'Well?' she asks as she stands before us, a vision of loveliness in champagne silk and lace, her wavy chestnut hair pinned up and adorned with a pearl tiara. She walks towards us and the dress moves with her like a second skin. It has a fitted bodice with lace sleeves that reach her wrists and the skirt falls from her waist to the floor where it seems to ripple and shimmer. It must be the light in here, probably designed to enhance the impact of these wedding dresses, but it's like Ava is wearing an actual silken waterfall.

The shop owner, Bella, a striking woman in her forties, or could be fifties, I can't really tell, claps her hands together and exclaims, 'That's the one! I knew it would be perfect for you.'

'I don't even want to try any others on,' Ava says. 'I feel like a princess.'

'And you look like one too,' Bella says. A voice at the back of my mind whispers that of course she wants to sell this dress to Ava because of the price tag, but then I admonish myself for being negative.

Bella moves around Ava, pinning where she thinks the dress needs to be taken in a fraction or taken up a touch, and I return to the sofa and sit with Nancy.

'What about you?' I ask. 'Are you going to look at the mother-of-the-bride outfits?'

A blush spreads up Nancy's neck and into her cheeks. 'I ... I don't know,' she whispers. 'It's quite ... expensive in here.'

'Edward's paying though?' I check even though I'm fairly certain that was agreed in the initial consultation with Edward and Ava. He said I was to spare no expense when shopping with his fiancée and her mother.

'I wish I could afford to pay for it myself,' Nancy says.

I can understand that. But this isn't about me and what I want, it's about my clients and so I plaster a wide smile on my face and say, 'Edward wants you to have the best, Nancy, so why don't we have a look at what's on offer here?'

She chews at her bottom lip before nodding. 'OK then, but I'm not rushing into anything. I want to check if I can get it cheaper somewhere else first.'

I give a small nod, knowing that once Nancy discovers something here, Bella will persuade her that she won't find it anywhere else and seal the deal. Bella is an excellent salesperson and she can be very convincing, so I accompany Nancy to the mother-of-the-bride section while Bella continues to make small adjustments to Ava's dress. It's important, I think, seeing how wonderful Ava looks, that Nancy has the right outfit and so I will also do my best to persuade her not to worry about money. After all, Edward has plenty to go round. He made sure to tell me that when he first approached me via my website and so I'm going to do what I can to make sure he's happy with everything.

---

AFTER LEAVING the wedding dress boutique, we wander around Covent Garden for a bit, admiring the flower displays and enjoying the fresh spring day. I find Ava and Nancy easy to be around.

'Shall we get something to eat?' Nancy asks. 'My treat.'

'Good idea, Mum.' Ava smiles. 'You hungry, Grace?'

'I am actually and I know a great little Italian place,' I reply.

When we're seated at a table in the restaurant, I feel myself relaxing. We order a bottle of Barolo and the server pours for us. I raise my glass, savouring the aromas of plums, leather, and violets, and the taste of spice and red fruits. It's delicious, silky smooth on my tongue, and I could easily drain the glass, but I set it down on the table. I'm working, after all, and need to remain professional, however nice Ava and her mum are.

'Thank you for your help today,' Ava says to me. Her cheeks have roses in them and her eyes are shining and I can't tell if it's from the wine or emotion.

'No need to thank me,' I say. 'It's my job.'

'But you're so kind and helpful.' Ava takes a sip of wine and it stains her lips dark red. 'I really appreciate it so much. Mum always taught me that you should thank people, whether it's their job or not. It's basic manners.'

'It's true.' Nancy nods. 'It's important to make people feel appreciated. There's enough unpleasantness in this world, so I've always taught my two that making people feel valued is important. Lots are far too quick to criticise when they could be kind and grateful instead.'

I look from mother to daughter, and warmth fills my chest. They're such nice people and I'm lucky to be working with them, to be getting paid to do this.

I clear my throat. 'So, are you happy with the dress?' I ask Ava. I know she is, but I want to check. Sometimes brides can change their mind. I secretly referred to one bride I worked with as a bridezilla because she changed her mind about the dress five times and, in the end, she wore three throughout the course of the day. Her parents absolutely doted her upon her so they were happy to spend hundreds of thousands on the dresses alone.

'I love it.' Ava nods. 'I never thought I'd ever have a dress like that.'

'Did you have a prom dress?' I ask. I didn't go to a prom, but I know they're quite popular with schools these days. It's a delightful idea being able to dress up and have a kind of send-off as you embark upon the next stage of your life.

Ava shakes her head. 'I didn't go to prom.'

I see Nancy shifting in her seat. 'She didn't tell me that there was a prom.'

'Why not?' I ask.

'I knew we couldn't afford for me to go and I didn't want Mum to feel bad, so I didn't tell her about it.'

My heart squeezes. Some teenagers would make their parents feel guilty about this, but not Ava. She didn't even tell her mum about it and that shows what a sweet person she was even back then.

'It wasn't just the dress,' she explains. 'It would have been all the added extras as well, like hair, makeup, nails, shoes, and transport. I know some girls at school spent a fortune on it, or it seemed like a fortune back then, and I knew we could never afford all that.'

'We'd have found a way,' Nancy says, shaking her head. 'I wish you'd told me. I still feel terrible about it.'

'Mum,' Ava says, placing a hand over one of Nancy's, 'It's fine. It's all a long time ago and I don't feel like I missed out. Besides which, look at the wedding dress I've just bought. It more than makes up for not going to prom.'

'I'm glad, love.' Nancy smiles, but there's sadness in her eyes. It must be hard being a mum and not being able to give your children everything they want.

A server arrives and takes our order, and when he's gone, Ava raises her glass. 'Here's to new beginnings and happy ever afters.'

'Cheers,' I clink my glass against hers and then Nancy's and drink. 'I swear this is the nicest red wine I've ever tasted.'

'It ought to be at that price.' Nancy snorts and the three of us laugh. 'Sorry, I'll stop talking about money now. I just think that if you've got it, you don't worry about it, but when you struggle financially, it can be all you think about.'

'I get that.' I nod, thinking about my situation and how I can't afford a place of my own.

'Tell us a bit about you, Grace,' Nancy says, reaching for a breadstick.

'Ummm ... like what?' I sit up straighter. Talking about myself is not my favourite pastime.

'Anything you like, dear,' she replies. 'No pressure.'

I sip my wine again, fortifying myself. 'I uhhh ... love my job.' *Did* love my job, before my heart was broken.

'I'm sure it's wonderful,' Nancy says dreamily. 'Planning people's big day and seeing them marry. It's meant to be the happiest day of someone's life, right? Although I still swear that the happiest days of my life were when I gave birth to Grace and then to Daniel. But you young women have all that to come, don't you?'

'Maybe, Mum, and maybe not. As you know, not every woman has to be a mother.' Ava shakes her head. 'For a start, it's not what every woman wants, and for those who do aspire to be mothers, it's not always achievable.'

'Especially without a man,' I add, wincing at my quick mouth. It gets away from me sometimes and I say things then wish I hadn't.

'It helps if there's a man around.' Nancy laughs and I relax again. I thought she might ask me about my romantic life and it's a topic I prefer to avoid if I can. After all, there's nothing that bursts someone's bubble like hearing a sad tale about love gone wrong. Most people go silent and an awkward grey cloud settles over the room. I don't want that for Ava and Nancy because they want me to create the perfect wedding, and how can they trust me to do that when my own story is so sad? It's not exactly a great advert for my business.

'Mum's been seeing Jeff,' Ava says with a grin.

'Ava!' Nancy shakes her head. 'That's not exactly true.'

'Oh, come on, Mum, we all know it is.'

'Jeff is a very nice man and we've been out for dinner a few times, that's all.' Nancy is blushing furiously now.

'Who's Jeff?' I ask.

'Sorry, I forgot you don't know,' Ava replies. 'Jeff Turnbull is Edward's driver.'

'I see.' I nod.

'We're not dating.' Nancy scowls at her daughter, but then

her lips twitch and she hides her smile behind her wine glass.

'All right, Mum, have it your way.' Ava gives an exaggerated wink, and it makes me giggle.

'What about you, Grace?' Nancy asks, and the smile drops from my face while the laughter dies in my throat.

'What about me?' I croak.

'Are you seeing anyone?' Nancy tilts her head.

'Mum! You shouldn't ask questions like that.' Ava sighs.

'It's OK.' I smile. 'But the answer's no. I'm far too busy for dating.'

That seems to satisfy them as a response and then, thankfully, our food arrives and we're otherwise occupied. It's good food too, just as I knew it would be. Rich tomato and garlic sauces, pasta perfectly cooked, and bright green side salads. We follow it with tiramisu that's light and fluffy but also rich and chocolaty, and laced with coffee liqueur.

'I'd better not eat like that too often over the next few weeks,' Ava says then drains her wine glass. 'I won't fit into my dress if I do.'

'Nor me.' Nancy grins. 'Food like that makes it worth it, though.'

I polish off my final spoon of tiramisu, not caring if I need to buy bigger trousers. No one sees me naked these days, so who gives a damn? Not that I haven't felt conscious of the extra pounds I've gained since I last stood naked in front of a man, but I'm trying to be positive about it. I'll never be Miss World and I'll never be comfortable in a swimsuit, but I can fill out a lacy bra with no padding and I'll never need butt implants. Well look at me go! It must be the wine giving me some confidence.

'Where shall we go next?' Ava asks after Nancy has paid the bill and refused to accept a penny from me or Ava. Instead, I leave a tip on the table. I find it impossible not to leave something because I know how hard service staff work.

'How about somewhere with pretty lingerie?' I ask. 'You'll need something for the big day and for the honeymoon.'

Ava giggles. 'Good plan!' Then she glances at Nancy. 'Sorry, Mum.'

Nancy waves a hand. 'Don't be sorry, my darling. Sex is an important part of a loving relationship and, of course, you want pretty lingerie under your wedding dress. Let's go and find you some.'

When we leave the restaurant, the air outside is fresh and cool on my warm cheeks and I realise how full my belly is, but it's nice. I enjoyed the food, wine and the company. If it wasn't for the fact that I'm carrying my laptop in my bag and have a mental checklist at the forefront of my brain, I could almost imagine that these two lovely women were my friends and we were out shopping for the day. But they're my clients, not my friends, and I'm working, so I need to remember that.

'Come on then,' I say, hitching my bag strap over my shoulder. 'I know just the place.'

I march on ahead and they follow me, arm in arm, chatting enthusiastically about the wedding day and the honeymoon that Edward has booked. I hope it's somewhere beautiful because Ava deserves to have the best honeymoon ever, and the more I hear about Edward, the more certain I am that it will be perfect. Edward knows how lucky he is and so does Ava, so they have every chance of having the happy ever after so many of us crave. Not me though. I'm here to ensure that other people's dreams come true and that's exactly what I'm going to do. I've abandoned all hope of a happy ever after of my own.

# Chapter 4

## *Jack*

'Lift your arm please, sir.' I do as the tailor asks, and he places the measuring tape under my armpit and stretches it along my arm. It tickles a tad and I breathe deeply to stay still and not collapse with laughter.

'Suits you, Jack.' Lucas sniggers and I flash him a warning glance.

Edward has got us at the tailor's on Saville Row to be fitted for tuxedos for the wedding. Thank fuck we're having black suits and not fancy morning suits with tails and top hats. That really would have been too much for me and for Lucas, although Lucas would have derived great pleasure from taking the piss out of me all day, I'm sure.

'We hitting the clubs tonight then?' Lucas asks. 'I could do with some pus—'

'Don't say it, Lucas!' Edward cuts him off. 'Remember where we are.'

'I was going to say I could do with some *push*-ups on the dance floor.' Lucas grins at Edward. 'I haven't strutted my stuff or bust a groove for a while, see?'

Edward shakes his head and rolls his eyes.

'You coming with us?' Lucas asks Edward.

'Not tonight.'

'Why not?' Lucas frowns. 'You never want to join the fun anymore.'

'He's happy now,' I say, watching Edward's face. 'Why would he want to come out and eat burgers when he has steak at home?'

Lucas guffaws. 'Steak at home? And burgers? More like prime pus—'

'Enough!' Edward scowls at Lucas and he sighs. 'Learn to toe the line, Lucas.'

'Sorry. I'm just fooling around. We know you're Mr Uptight now.'

'I'm not uptight,' Edward says. 'Being happy, I don't feel the need to go strutting my stuff around a club. I like a night out as much as the next man, but your idea of a good night out involves a lot of ... strutting.' He glowers at Lucas.

'It's all harmless fun.' Lucas shrugs.

'Until someone gets hurt.' Edward pushes a hand through his dark hair. 'You know I have Joe and Ava to think about now, and what with the wedding planning, I don't have time to waste on getting drunk, let alone on hangovers.'

'You don't know what you're missing,' Lucas says.

'That's the thing though ... I do know and I don't miss it.' Edward holds up a tie and peers at it. 'I have what I want and I will not risk it, ever. You still live like a young, single man without a care in the world.'

'I am a young, single man.' Lucas laughs. 'Young, single, and ready to mingle. You'll be there though, right?' he says to me.

'Yeah, I'll join you. I don't have a gorgeous fiancée and young son at home waiting for me.'

'Thank fuck for that.' Lucas nods slowly. 'I lost one best friend to cosy domesticity and I would hate to lose another.'

We spend the rest of the afternoon being fitted for suits and then head to a bar for a celebratory drink. Edward agreed to come for one before he heads home to Ava and Joe and it's nice to have some time just the three of us. I missed this when Edward was grieving for his first wife, Lucille. He locked himself away in his country home for two years and would only see a few people during that time. He still worked and ran Cavendish Construction remotely, but he was like a ghost of the man we'd known. Lucas took it particularly hard, and I felt like I had to be there for both of them, supporting Edward in whatever way I could and being there to soothe Lucas when he felt dejected. It wasn't an easy time at all, especially with lockdown too, but we got through it and I know these two men would do anything for me just as I would for them. We've been friends since university and we've been through a lot. But such is the way life goes sometimes. Not many of us escape unscathed and no one gets out of this alive, so we do what we can to make it as bearable as possible. Of course, I've had my share of heartache, but I push that to one side whenever it crosses my mind because I'm not one to dwell on the sad stuff. What's the point? Life is short and all that, right?

'Shall we get a round of shots?' Lucas asks.

'You can do what you like, but count me out.' Edward downs his beer then stands up.

'Stay for one more, won't you?' Lucas stares at Edward and I watch as our friend weighs things up. 'It's not like you have to drive and Jack and I feel like we barely see you these days.'

'I do what I can,' Edward replies.

'I know, but we miss you.' Lucas looks over at the bar and waves to get the attention of the bartender.

'All right, one more, but then I'm going. Jeff needs to get home, too.'

'To see his lady friend?' Lucas waggles his eyebrows. He told me he saw Jeff and Ava's mother at a restaurant, and they looked very cosy. I think it's nice that Edward's driver and his future mother-in-law are getting on well. It'll be just like one big happy family round at his estate.

'One more.' Edward holds up a finger, ignoring Lucas' comment about Nancy and Jeff, but I can see laughter in his eyes and that he's pretty happy that things are going well for Jeff too.

The round of shots soon arrives and we clink the glasses together, then throw them back, each of us wincing as the liquid burns on its way down.

'To love and marriage,' Lucas says as he raises another glass. 'May it be everything you want it to be, Edward, and may Jack and I always remain happy and free.'

'I'll drink to that,' I say as I take another shot and down it like my life depends upon it.

## Chapter 5

## *Grace*

'You look hot tonight, girl!'

I flash a grin at Freddie. 'Why thanks, doll, so do you.'

He takes my hand and twirls me around to the Abba classic, making my red silk dress shift over my skin like a whisper, and my head spins. It was a busy week with work and I'm tired but glad I made the effort to come out with my friends Freddie and Toni. Sometimes what a girl needs is a night out with her mates and a bloody good dance.

From the corner of my eye, I spot Toni waving at us, so I grab Freddie's hand and lead him over to her. 'Toni's got another round in.'

The prices at this club make me wince, but that's London life for you. We usually have a few wines together before we come out to save money because a round of cocktails here costs almost as much as a semi-decent bottle of champagne at a supermarket. However, this evening I met my friends here because I had some work to finish first. I definitely couldn't afford to do this every night or even every weekend, but it's worth it now and then to spend the evening with these two lovely friends of mine.

We perch on stools at the table Toni grabbed for us and I tuck my small bag under my thigh. It's warm in the club and I reach for my drink, take a sip and shiver. 'Wow! That's strong,' I say.

'It ought to be for the bloody price.' Toni giggles. 'Cheers, my dears.'

Despite being twenty-eight, she could easily pass for eighteen with her pink hair that falls in waves to her waist, her peaches and cream complexion, and pale blue eyes. She has a small nose piercing on the left side and earrings that run all the way up her ears, as well as other piercings she has told me about, but I haven't seen because they are in more intimate places. Her loud laugh never fails to warm my heart and she's the most relaxed person I've ever met. I could spend hours just gazing at the tattoos that run up her arms and across her neck because she's like a walking, talking work of art.

'How's the shop doing?' I ask her.

'Really well.' She nods. 'Just had my best week ever, actually.'

She opened a boho clothing shop in Camden a few years ago. It's a charming place with vintage and sustainable clothing, and occasionally other random items. I love going there because it's colourful and cosy and always smells of incense and coffee. I had one bride get her dress from there because she wanted a sustainable piece and Toni had just had a trunk of old wedding dresses delivered. Toni lives in a shared house ten minutes from the shop and still acts like a university student in many ways. I don't think I could cope with that at my age, but Toni enjoys sharing her space with others and is in no rush to hop on the property ladder or to settle down.

'That's amazing news.' I raise my glass. 'Cheers to that.'

The three of us clink glasses.

'How about you, Freddie?'

'I have another celebrity client.' He wiggles his eyebrows.

'Oooh! Can you name them?' I ask, my interest piqued. As a personal trainer with an excellent reputation, he works with a wide variety of people and has several celebrity clients on his books.

'I shouldn't, but hey ... I know you won't say a word. You know that new ITV drama with the body found in the attic?'

'I know it.' In fact, I was glued to it, along with Maisie and Riya.

'Well ... it's the actress who plays the younger version of the woman who was found in the attic.'

'Wow! You live such a glamorous life.' I wink at him and he throws back his head and laughs.

'I know right.'

'Grace!' Toni taps my arm, but she's looking across the club.

'What's up?'

'That guy hasn't taken his eyes off you.'

'What guy?'

'Him.' She nods toward a group of men and I try to focus on them, but the club is dark and people keep walking past and obscuring my view.

I squint a bit and then I see him.

And he is staring at me or ... I turn around to see if maybe he's staring at someone behind me, but no ... he's staring right at me.

And he is drop dead fucking gorgeous.

I slide off my stool, grab my bag, then head for the toilets, needing to get myself away from those intense dark eyes before they bore a hole right through me.

# Chapter 6

## *Jack*

'Earth to Jack!' Lucas taps me on the shoulder, then on the chest, then on the side of my head, albeit lightly.

'What is it?' I shrug him off without looking at him.

'What are you staring at?'

Lucas places his head next to mine and bursts into laughter. 'Ahhhhh ... nice.'

That grabs my attention, and I turn to him. 'I saw her first.'

He holds up his hands and shakes his head. 'Hey, hey, I'm not going to encroach upon the object of your lust, man.'

'Shut the fuck up.' I growl in my throat, a warning, but it makes him laugh harder.

'Got you bad, has she?' he asks.

I look back across the club, but the woman has gone. 'Fuck! Where'd she go?' I scan the club, but I can't see her. Her companion with the pink hair and the tall, wiry man are still at the table though, so I'm hoping she hasn't gone home. That would be a tragedy.

'She's attractive enough, I guess,' I say to Lucas and his lips curve upwards. This man seems to be permanently grinning these days and I swear it's because he's laughing at me or Edward most of the time.

'Relax, bud. She went towards the toilets. She'll be back soon, I'm sure.' Lucas presses a beer into my hand. 'Drink this and get yourself together.'

'Did you see her, though?'

'She was all right if you like that sort of thing.'

'Lucas ... she was ...' What was she? Petite, but curvy in a way that gave me an instant erection. Those hips, those thighs in that red silk dress ... Those breasts, full, and round and I bet she has perfect nipples surrounded by silky soft areola just perfect for sucking. Will they be pale or dark pink? My cock twitches in anticipation and I haven't even spoken to her yet. As far as I can tell in the dim light of the club, her hair that tumbles down her back in waves is blonde. Her eyes were light but I couldn't tell what colour from this distance. I already know that I want to take her home with me tonight. I want to take her home and strip her naked and devour that perfect body, do things to her that make her beg for more. Or for mercy from the pleasure gods...

'Pink hair is staring at you,' Lucas mutters.

It might be dark, but you can't miss the fact that her hair is pink because it's basically luminous.

'Do you think the cuffs match the collar?' Lucas asks.

'It's not her I'm interested in. It's blondie,' I reply, and Lucas chuckles.

And then I spot her, weaving her way through the crowd, hips swaying, hair like a golden waterfall.

Everything happens in slow motion.

A guy carrying a tray of drinks stumbles and staggers, most likely drunk.

He crashes into her, and she's thrown off balance.

She throws up her hands, but it's too late ... she's falling ... falling ...

And I'm running. Running.

And then ...

# Chapter 7

## *Grace*

Strong arms catch me before I hit the floor. A strangled scream escapes me. I'm pulled against a strong, hard chest and I hear a deep voice booming expletives in the direction of the guy who knocked me flying. When he's finished, his hands gently move up my back and then take hold of my upper arms and move me backwards so I can peer up into his face.

*It's him.* Beardy guy with the intense eyes.

'Hey,' he says. 'You OK?'

I nod, mutely, my chest heaving. My eyes roam over his thick beard, sculpted cheekbones, full lips, and broad shoulders like I'm desperate to see all of him before he walks away. This has to be a dream, surely? He just saved me from getting hurt by catching me in his arms like some kind of real-life superhero.

'Take it easy a moment,' he says kindly, and I rest my head against him again. He smells so good, expensive and masculine, and the image of licking his neck darts through my mind.

What is wrong with me?

*Cut it out!*

A warm hand cups my chin, and he raises my head so he can gaze into my eyes.

'Can I get you something? A glass of water? Something stronger?'

*How about you, naked?*

'Uhhh ... water would be great, thanks.'

'No problem.'

He leads me over to the table where Toni and Freddie are halfway out of their seats, like they were about to rush over to me, but then changed their minds. Beardy guy helps me onto my stool then says, 'I'll be right back.'

When he's gone in the direction of the bar, Toni grabs my right hand. 'You OK?'

'I think so.'

'He was like some kind of superhero then,' Freddie says. 'I've never seen a guy move that quickly.'

'He practically flew in and caught you,' Toni says. 'He must have superpowers.'

A giggle slips out. 'He's cute, right?'

'Pretty frigging hot, Grace,' Toni replies. 'And he's gone to get you a drink.'

'I know.' I look over at the bar and watch as my hero gets me a bottle of water and a glass, then brings it back to the table. He opens it in front of me, a gesture I appreciate because I never accept drinks from strangers. You never know if someone might drug them, right?

He pours the water into the glass, then hands it to me and I take a sip. It's cold and refreshing so I drink some more.

'Better?' he asks.

'Much.'

'I'm just going to powder my nose,' Toni says, flashing me a meaningful stare.

'Me too.' Freddie gets up and they leave the table.

'Can I get you anything else?' beardy guy asks.

'How about your name?' I smile, but inwardly I curse myself. What am I doing flirting? The last thing I need is to get involved in something, even if it's just a flirtation.

'How about you try to guess my name and I'll let you know if you're right?' He cocks an eyebrow in a way that makes my core clench hungrily. Well, it has been a while...

'You want to guess mine?' I say, playfully.

He purses his full lips for a moment, then says, 'How about if we choose a name for each other? Just for fun.'

'I'm up for that,' I reply. *Who even am I this evening?*

'OK then ... I think you could be ... Goldilocks.'

'Goldilocks?' I laugh. 'You think I look like someone who'd

break into a cottage, steal porridge, break chairs, then sleep in other people's, or rather bears', beds?'

'I think you could be capable of doing anything you choose.' He's leaning on the table now and my eyes roam over his forearms, exposed by his rolled-up shirt sleeves. He has tattoos that lead up from his wrists and disappear under his shirt. I wonder how far they go.

'I'll take Goldilocks, but maybe shorten it to Goldie?'

'I can do that.' He nods, then runs his left hand over his beard. 'What do you want to call me?'

Making up names for strangers in clubs is not something I'd usually do, but it's been such a long time since I've flirted with a man. This guy is hot and playful and I'm tired of being so guarded all the time, so I figure, what's the harm?

'I think you could be called ... Mountain Man.'

'Mountain Man?' His eyes crinkle at the corners. 'Because of my beard?'

'And your build.' I stare at his broad shoulders and muscular arms and heat pulses between my legs. 'You look like you could handle yourself in the mountains.'

'What? While wrestling bears?'

'I guess so.'

Oh my god, I'm really laying it on thick now and realise I'm even tilting my head and batting my eyelashes at him. How many drinks have I had?

'Tell you what, I'll wrestle those bears for you while you slip between the sheets of the most comfortable bed and then maybe I'll join you,' he says.

*Wow! Just wow!* Where is this going?

'How about you call me Mounty then and I'll call you Goldie?'

'How about Bear?' The more I look at him with that beard and those brown eyes, the more I can imagine him growling as he wrestles me to the ground. His strength overpowering me as I gaze up at him and feel his big, hard co—

'Bear and Goldie?' He snaps me out of my risqué reverie. 'Deal?'

'Deal.' I hold out my hand for him to shake but he takes it between both of his and raises it to his lips. As he kisses my hand, his beard tickles and when his tongue darts out and licks between my fingers, I gasp. He finishes with a gentle nip at the pad between the thumb and forefinger of my right hand, and I know I'm going to imagine this when I next use my vibrator. This guy is the stuff of fantasies. The problem is, I bet he knows it.

'What are your plans for the rest of the night?' he asks.

I try to swallow, but it's like all the moisture in my body has gone south and I can feel it soaking into my panties.

'I ... I'm not sure.' I glance over towards the toilets and see Toni and Freddie pretending to speak to each other while casting what they think are discreet glances my way.

'You fancy getting out of here and heading to my place?' he asks.

'Oh ... I don't normally make a habit of leaving clubs with strange men.' *Dammit!*

'Tell you what,' he says. 'How about I give your friends my number and my address and then they'll know where you are?'

That idea makes me feel like I'm about sixteen, but I also know there's no point taking risks. 'Hang on.'

I retrieve my phone from my bag and activate the location-sharing app then message Toni and Freddie to let them know.

'I'll just pop over to them and tell them we're leaving,' I say.

*OMG! Am I really going to do this?*

'Great.' He gently brushes a thumb over my cheek and follows it with a kiss. 'You'll be in safe hands, I promise.'

My eyes appraise his hands: big, strong, capable. They look like hands that can provide pleasure and anticipation makes my stomach flip over.

Taking a deep breath, I slide off the stool. I can't believe this is me, but it's been so long since I've been with a man and this man is truly gorgeous, well dressed and judging by the expensive watch on his left wrist, he has money too. I never take chances, never, but I'll let my friends know what's happening and they can monitor my location. Plus, it's exciting doing something I wouldn't normally consider. What is it they say about regrets? You only regret the chances you don't take? I'm not an adventurous person but sometimes I get fed up with being me, of never taking chances because I'm so afraid of getting hurt, of letting go.

Tonight, however, it seems like I'm going to take a chance. Well, Goldilocks is anyway. Tonight I'll leave Grace behind and be the woman I'd like to be. Goldie takes what she wants and I'm up for having me some of that.

My body is already quivering with desire while my heart is thundering with nerves.

*No more regrets, Goldilocks! Go grab your bear!*

# Chapter 8

## *Grace*

Outside the club, Bear takes my hand. 'I'll call my driver,' he says.

'You have a driver?' My voice rises in question, and I cough to clear my throat.

'Yes.' He laughs softly. 'But I don't use him all the time. It's handy for after a night out though and for when I need to conduct meetings or work on the way to the office.'

'Right.' I nod as if I understand and do this all the time, too. Oh to have a driver so I could work in the car. Instead, I'm limited to working on the bus or train and at *Cupcake Corner*, my unofficial office.

'Were your friends all right with you leaving with me?' he asks.

'They were fine, but they will watch the app all night and probably expect hourly texts from me to reassure them I'm safe.'

'You can FaceTime them on the hour every hour if you like,' he says. 'Although ... we might have to make sure to keep the calls short.'

'Why's that?' I ask, breathless.

'I have plans for us.'

'You do?' I have to make an effort to shut my mouth. Yes, he's hot and seemingly rich and he smells like heaven, but he could be a flop in bed. God only knows I've had a few of those over the years. Before the last one, that was, because there's been no one since him and he wasn't exactly a selfless lover. He was more *wham, bam, I refuse to thank you, ma'am, because I'm rolling over to go to sleep*. I even wondered if that was normal behaviour for a man in a relationship and so I put up with it, grateful for scraps from his table, grateful for the rare orgasm he gave me when he could be bothered to make sex last. This guy could be exactly the same and then I'll be disappointed. Or will I? Perhaps it will simply be another nail in the coffin of my dating history. After all, I've been with a *clunk click every trip*, as I thought of one of my former lovers. He was very jerky and would pounce, penetrate and quickly come, leaving me not even remotely warmed up. Then there was the guy who wouldn't get his tongue out of my mouth. It was a small poky tongue, and I tried everything to get him to keep it in his mouth. He was a few years older, and I thought he'd be more knowledgeable and experienced, but no, he thought it was all about sticking his tongue in my mouth and poking it around. If only he'd tried that further down my body, but he told me he didn't like 'doing that' because it wasn't his thing. We shagged twice, and that was enough. I still shudder when I think about that invasive, poky tongue. There were a few others, but nothing that made me come as hard as my vibrator and my imagination do. Those I can rely on. In fact, if this guy is shit in bed, I'm investing in a new vibrator and some erotica and men can go do one.

A black limousine pulls up at the kerb and Bear says, 'This is us.'

'You have a limo?'

He shrugs. 'It's a company car.'

'That doesn't make it any less glamorous.' Not that I haven't been with a man with money, of course, but I also learnt that money doesn't make a good man. I'm not sure what does, to be honest.

The driver gets out and comes around and opens the door and Bear gestures for me to get in. I do then I hear him say something to the driver before he gets in too.

Suddenly, panic overwhelms me. I'm acting like a different person and I need to go home, drink some water and get some sleep. I can laugh at this crazy behaviour tomorrow and wonder what on earth I was thinking.

Bear slides along the leather seat towards me and takes my hand. 'Hey ... Are you OK? We can drive you straight home if you like. There's no pressure for you to come home with me.'

His eyes are kind yet mischievous, as if he's daring me to make the wild decision. His smile is warm yet wicked, like he's part angel, part devil.

He turns my hand over in his and runs a finger over the palm. 'Round and round the garden, like a growly bear ...'

He meets my gaze and grins. 'One step.' He walks his fingers up my arm and my nipples tighten. 'Two steps.' He walks the fingers to my shoulder and across my collar bones. A sigh escapes me. 'Kiss me right there.' He leans forwards and kisses me so softly on the mouth it's like feathers being stroked across my lips.

'No,' I say, and he leans back, his brows meeting.

'No?' He nods. 'That's fine. We'll take you straight home.'

'No!' I reply sharply. 'I meant, no, don't take me home. Take me with you ... please.'

The privacy screen is up between us and the driver, so when Bear turns me to face him, then kisses me again, I relax into it. He kisses me gently at first, but then he places his hands either side of my face and his kisses deepen. His tongue tangles with mine and I moan with desire, yearning for him to touch me. When his hands slide down and roam over my breasts where there's only silk and lace between us, I almost explode with need. It has been an age since a man touched me and I'm desperate for more. He cups my breasts as if he's weighing them, then he squeezes my nipples in a way that makes something deep inside me respond.

*Fuck, this is good!*

'I want to look at you.' He places a hand on my chest and pushes me backwards until I'm lying on the seat. He parts my legs then he pushes my skirt up my thighs. Shyness overwhelms me and I stop his hands.

'What is it?' he asks.

'I'm ... self-conscious.'

*Healing the Billionaire's Heart*

'Don't be. You're exquisite and I want to see you.'

I pause for a moment then move my hands above my head, exhale slowly to relax myself and he pushes my dress up to my hips. While he stares at my lace panties, there's something about the awe and wonder in his eyes that turns me on even more. I enjoy being wanted like this, being brazen, being Goldie.

'Your thighs are so soft and round,' he says, his voice thick with lust. 'I love your curves. And this ass.' He cups my behind and squeezes it hard. 'It's so sexy. I want to fuck you from behind and watch as it jiggles.'

Still cupping my bottom with one hand, he moves the other round and strokes it over the lace covering my mound. He slides the tip of his finger down, down, so it tickles my clit and my folds through the material. When he looks up, he holds my gaze as he keeps moving that finger and then it slips beneath the lace.

Skin meets skin.

Electricity sparks.

My back arches.

He adds another finger and they both roam my folds, slide along either side of my swollen clit, building sensation and speed.

'Touch your breasts,' he says, and I do without hesitation. I cup and squeeze through the silk and he keeps caressing my most sensitive place. As he moves his other hand around and penetrates me with two thick fingers, I instinctively move my hips, intensifying the pleasure.

'What do you want?' he asks. 'Tell me.'

'Make me come.'

'Beg me.' His voice is stern, in command.

'Please, Bear, make me come.'

'Your wish is my command,' he growls, then he speeds up his caresses while his fingers fuck me hard.

Sensation builds and builds and I ride him without shame or embarrassment. My core clenches around him until I can't take it anymore and I shatter into a million pieces, crying out his fake name.

'That's my girl,' he says. 'Good little Goldilocks. You're golden down here too and so beautiful.' Then he does something no man has ever done in front of me before. He puts the fingers that were inside me in his mouth and sucks them. 'You taste so fucking good.'

When he rearranges my underwear and my dress then helps me to sit up, I am in shock. I have never orgasmed like that with a man before. It's strange though because I came so hard and yet I want more. Is this what happens when you meet someone you really desire? When the so-called chemistry is right?

'Would you like me to...' I nod at his groin, and he takes my hand and places it there. Through the fabric of his trousers, I can feel an enormous erection, bigger than anything I've ever felt before. I want to see it and feel it inside me.

'I can wait.' He steals a kiss and nips at my bottom lip. 'It'll be worth it.'

When the car stops and the driver opens the door, I make to stand up, but my legs are shaky. Bear wraps his arm around my waist and takes my hand in his, then he helps me out of the limousine. As we walk towards the building, I think that if I'm like this after he only touched me with his fingers, what will I be like after he's fucked me with his cock?

# Chapter 9

## *Jack*

We take the lift to my apartment and it's all I can do not to push Goldie against the wall, lift her dress, pull that scrap of lace aside and fuck her hard.

Around us our reflections keep us company in the mirrored lift walls, and I imagine opening the front of her wrap dress and exposing those big tits, turning her around and watching as they bounce while I take her from behind.

My cock is throbbing with raw animal need, but I wait. I know it's better to wait because it will be worth it when I get her inside my home because then I can take her every which way I want.

Watching her come on my fingers, the way she was initially shy but then overwhelmed by desire, was delightful. And she wasn't faking it either, like some women I've known in my time. Despite my efforts, some feel the need to ham it up instead of simply enjoying the moment. But Goldie took what she wanted, what she needed, and she came all over my hands.

She's soaking now and it will make what I'm going to do to her later all the sweeter because she's lubricated by her own sweet juices. I can't wait to make her orgasm again and again and again.

# Chapter 10

## *Grace*

The lift doors open into Bear's apartment, and I press my lips together to stop myself gasping because it's gorgeous. This man must have serious money, either that or he's house-sitting for someone with serious money.

A kitchen diner is connected to the large open-plan lounge. Hardwood floors are polished to a sheen, and the floor to ceiling windows boast views that stretch out over London. The space is low-lit with lamps and I wonder if the windows have privacy glass so he can see out but people can't see in.

'Do you want a drink?' he asks.

'Yes, please. And could I use the bathroom?'

'Sure. Along the hallway and it's the first door on the right.'

'Thanks.'

I kick off my shoes, leaving them near the lift doors and head along the corridor, opening the first door. The light comes on automatically. In the bathroom, a mixture of citrus and ginger fills the air, accompanied by a slight trace of bleach. Honey-coloured tiles cover the walls and floor, and there is a large walk-in shower, a clawfoot tub, and his and hers sinks. Shutters cover the window and an activated extractor fan hums, presumably triggered when the lights came on.

I use the toilet, wash my hands, and lightly dab tissues on my cheeks to preserve my makeup.

Meeting my eyes in the mirror above the sinks, I shake my head. This is not me. I do not go home with strange men, however gorgeous they are. My eyes are shiny, my pupils dilated and my cheeks rosy. I look wild and wanton. There's a rosy hue across my chest too, and my nipples are still hard beneath the silky fabric of my dress and the lace of my bra. What just happened in the limo was explosive. I can't believe I let a virtual stranger touch me and gaze at my most private parts, and yet it totally turned me on. I don't even know his real name but it seems to have helped me to find a new sexual height that I haven't previously reached. The anonymity of it, the fact that I can be whoever I want to be and don't have to 'stick to a type' is exciting and liberating. Being a woman often entails playing various roles: daughter, wife, niece, mother, friend, lover. This evening I can shrug all of that away and be the person I want to be. I can priori tise my own needs instead of being controlled by societal expectations. I've never done this before and I'll probably never do it again, but for one night, I'm going to have some no-strings fun.

After firing off texts to Toni and Freddie to let them know we've arrived safely, I tuck my phone back in my bag, shake out my hair and apply some gloss to my lips. I'm a bit nervous but my dominant emotion is excitement about what the night will involve.

*Here I go...*

In the lounge, Bear is sitting in the corner of the large cream leather sofa. He's nursing a crystal tumbler of an amber liquid and he watches me as I walk towards him. He's so beautiful it takes my breath away. I pause at the end of the sofa to steady myself, set my bag down on the coffee table, and attempt a smile.

'I poured you a bourbon. Is that OK?' He gestures at the tumbler on the table.

'Great, thanks.' I pick up the glass and take a swig and it burns my tongue, then warms me inside as I swallow. I'm not much of a spirit drinker unless they're in cocktails, but I could do with something strong to give me courage.

'Are you going to sit down?' he asks me, a smile playing across his lips.

'Of course.' I lower myself onto the sofa, a whole seat between us. I need to gather my thoughts a moment because otherwise I have a feeling this will all happen too quickly.

'How are you feeling?' he asks.

'I'm OK.'

'Are you sure?'

I nod.

'Have you messaged your friends? To let them know you're safe?'

'Yes.'

He drains his glass, then places it on the table, stands up and unbuttons his shirt. He throws it to the chair in the corner, then turns to me and my heart pounds. His chest is broad and sculpted, with a spattering of dark hair that runs down his belly and beneath his trousers. He has defined abs and his trousers are low slung so I can see those muscles men get that run towards the groin as if they're signposting the best bit. I'm sure I've heard them called the Adonis belt, but whatever they're called, my mouth is watering.

Gazing at him, I realise how hungry I am. How hungry I've been for most of my life. I have never felt this way, never been so filled with the heat of desire as I am now. I've been attracted to men, sure, but I was always conscious of how handsome and rich some of them were, of how they wanted me to be a certain way — nurturing, understanding, practically maternal at times. It can be hard to unite those versions of me with a sexual being. But here, tonight, I'm free to be whatever I want without the need to be what Bear's looking for, because after tonight, we'll probably never see each other again.

I take a swig of my drink, then set the glass on the table, stand up and tug at the tie belt of my dress. The belt slips from my hand, the dress falls open and I stand there, waiting to see how Bear reacts.

'Fuck!' His upper lip curls and I see a flash of perfect white teeth. 'You are gorgeous.'

He steps forwards and his hands grip my waist then slide under the dress. He runs them up and down my sides, then up and over my shoulders before pushing the dress away.

The material floats down to the floor where it pools and I am in front of him, wearing just my lacy black balconette bra and panties.

Bear leans forwards and kisses me softly while running his hands over my back in a way that makes me weak. When his hands come around to my front and drift over my breasts, I moan. He caresses them gently, then tickles my hard nipples with the tips of his fingers before pinching them repeatedly in a rhythm that makes my core pulse. I can't take it anymore, so I unfasten the bra myself and drop it to the sofa.

'Perfection!' He lowers his head and sucks at my breasts and I cradle his head, wishing I had him inside of me, where I am aching with need.

He unzips his trousers and kicks them off, then his trunks follow and he's naked, his huge cock bouncing free, his balls pulled tight to his body. Seeing the bead of pre-cum, I kneel before him and take the tip into my mouth and run my tongue over it. He tastes so good and I move my head up and down, keen to take as much of him into my mouth as I can. Groaning, he winds his fingers into my hair and tilts my head back. I try to relax my mouth, but he's so big that my jaw aches with the effort of taking him deeper.

His cock pulses, and without warning, he pulls out.

'I don't want to come yet,' he says. 'On your knees on the sofa facing the window.'

While I get into position, he picks up his trousers and pulls a condom from the pocket, then rolls it on. When he kneels behind me, my stomach rolls with anticipation. Will I be able to take him? That cock is enormous.

'I bet you're still wet,' he says, leaning against me, then he slides a hand between my legs and proves his point. 'Fucking soaking.' His fingers find my clit and he rubs them up and down, round and round, and my desire rises again. 'Now I'm going to fuck you, Goldie, so I hope you're ready.'

'I'm ready.' My voice is almost a whimper. 'I can't wait!'

I meet his eyes in the window, and he smiles. Lust fills his eyes and it makes me feel sexy and powerful. This man wants me and he's going to take me.

The tip of his cock finds my entrance, and he slides in and out, deeper every time. As he enters me, I gasp because he stretches and fills me so completely that I realise I've never been penetrated like this before.

'Keep your head up,' he commands and I do, watching as he speeds up, pumping into me with such force that my breasts bounce. He has his hands on my hips, pulling me back towards him then pushing me forwards. He has total control and it thrills me to submit this to him. When he slows his thrusting, he reaches around and places his hands over my sex and then he starts to pump faster. The movement makes me bump against his hand and soon I'm at the edge of the abyss of pleasure. I pause there for a moment, waiting for bliss, and then I hurtle over the edge, pure explosive pleasure radiating through my clit, my core, and my whole body. Bear's climax comes straight after mine and it triggers another intense orgasm, this time deeper within me, as if he has unlocked a hidden treasure. I push back onto him, eking out the last ripples of my orgasm, and then I am spent.

Bear pulls out of me and gets off the sofa, then he reaches for me and helps me to my feet. 'Come with me,' he says.

In the hallway, he opens a door to a bedroom with two lamps and a king-sized bed. 'Get comfy and I'll join you in a moment.'

I cross the room and slide under the covers, sighing as comfort envelops me. The sheets are cool and soft against my warm skin and I lie there, dazed after the most explosive sex I've ever had. I didn't even believe it was possible to come twice in one session, let alone like that, with an internal orgasm. This man is a sex god and I am happy to worship at his temple.

When Bear returns wearing his trunks again, he's carrying two glasses of water. I watch as he approaches the bed, then sets a glass on the table next to me. 'Drink. You need to stay hydrated.'

'Thanks.' I sit up and take a long drink of the water and drain half the glass.

Bear goes around to the other side of the bed and sets his glass down, then gets in and slides towards me. He looks at me intently, and I wonder if he wants to go again. I don't know if I have the energy just now, but I don't want to look a gift horse in the mouth either. But he holds his arms open and I move into his embrace, then he turns me around and tucks me against him. 'Get some rest, Goldie.'

Lying in his muscular arms, I feel warm and content and soon I am drifting away on a postcoital cloud. My body and mind have never felt so calm and relaxed and my last thought before it all goes blank is that tomorrow, it will be hard to say goodbye when this man has just awakened things in me that have never been roused before.

'Goodnight, Bear,' I whisper.

'Night, Goldilocks.'

He kisses my neck, then buries his face in my hair and we fall asleep together.

# Chapter 11

## *Jack*

The next morning, I wake up from such a deep sleep that it feels like I was drugged the night before. Don't get me wrong, I have my fair share of sex, but fucking Goldilocks was ... pretty extraordinary. It's happened before, once or twice, that I've slept with a woman I find a connection with and the chemistry can be explosive. Goldilocks and I have good chemistry for sure. What a shame, then, that we won't see each other again.

My cock is hard and I realise it's because she's straddling my thighs, her wet pussy dripping over me, her hair sleep-mussed, her breasts heavy and round as she gyrates.

'Wait!' I reach for the bedside table and open the drawer without moving away from her, then pull out a roll of condoms. I give one to her and she opens it and slides it down my shaft, giving me a few firm strokes while holding my balls in her other hand.

When she stops, I groan, but then she takes my hands and pushes them above my head. I don't resist because I like this about her; she can be in control of her own pleasure because it turns me on even more. She feathers kisses down my chest, licks my nipples, then moves up my body and positions her pussy over my cock. Rotating her hips, she gets me to her opening without using her hands and then slides me inside tantalisingly slowly.

She takes me deeper, but when I try to touch her, she pushes my arms away. 'No touching until you absolutely can't bear it, Bear!' She winks.

As she rides me, her heavy tits sway, making me want to grab them, cover them with my mouth and suck them hard. She moves up and down, round and round, and the sensation builds. I can't take anymore and I reach for her tits, squeeze them so she cries out and leans forwards and her pussy clenches my cock hard as she comes.

Grabbing her hips, I flip her over, raise her legs against my shoulders and rest her bottom against my thighs. I can feel every inch of my cock buried deep inside her now and it's so good.

'Fuck me hard, Bear,' she begs, so I do.

I pump that tight little pussy hard while rubbing my right thumb over her clit, and she screams as she comes again, then I pulse into her, filling her with every drop I have to give.

When I lie down next to her, something washes over me and I have an unsettling feeling deep in my guts. This ... connection I felt. It's fucking terrifying. Normally, the morning after, I can't wait to get a woman out of my home, but with Goldilocks, it's different. I'm already feeling anxious about the knowledge that she's going to leave and I'm never going to see her again.

I need to get a grip because this isn't me. I don't fall for the women I fuck, and they don't (or are not supposed to) fall for me. Sex is a purely physical act, a release, and it can't ever be anything more for me. So, I summon the ice walls from my depths and rebuild them around my heart. However much Goldie might have got to me, I can't allow myself to fall for her. The rules are there for a reason.

# Chapter 12

## *Grace*

Sitting in the limousine alone, I lace my fingers together and try not to think about what Bear did to me on this very seat last night. My body feels exhausted from all the sex (lol), and sitting on hard seats for the next few days is going to be troublesome, that's for sure. We took a shower together and while I soaped myself; I noticed that I have tiny bruises on my thighs and bottom from where Bear held me so tight. That sent a thrill through me because I've never had sex bruises before. *What a night!* Of course, in the shower, we couldn't resist each other and so we had sex in there too. Bear picked me up and wrapped my legs around his waist and fucked me against the tiles and I swear it was so hot I came within seconds. He has condoms available in every drawer of the apartment and it made me wonder if he does this all the time, but I quickly brushed the thought away because it doesn't matter; last night was a one off and what he does is none of my business.

He offered me breakfast, but I didn't want to overstay my welcome, so I made an excuse about having plans with family and he told me his driver would take me home. At the lift, he kissed me softly and despite my knowledge that it was a one-night stand; I swear my heart fractured a little, knowing I'd never see him or kiss him again. But that's the sentimental side of me and if we'd gone into last night expecting and wanting more, then it might not have been as hot. So … deep breaths and moving forwards … that's what I need to do. I know one thing for sure though, I'll never forget last night.

I message Toni and Freddie then Maisie — I told her I was staying at Toni's last night to avoid any awkward conversations — then I tuck my phone back in my bag and rest my head against the seat.

I am spent.

I am sated.

And I wish I could do it all over again.

Later on, I'm in the café with Maisie and Riya. They've closed for the day, but the tables are laden with plates of cakes ready for a cake tasting session.

'These look amazing,' I say to Riya and she smiles.

'I hope they like them.' She goes to the door and peers out onto the street. It's just past five and it's still light out. I can see through the window that the sky is painted prettily with pink and apricot hues. 'There they are!'

She unlocks the door and opens it.

*Healing the Billionaire's Heart*

Soon, Ava and Edward appear along with Edward's young son, Joe.

'Good evening.' Riya greets them and welcomes them inside.

After we've all said our hellos, Ava, Edward, and Joe sit at a table and I join them with Riya while Maisie makes drinks.

'Goodness, Edward, where do we start?' Ava asks, a shy smile gently curving her lips.

'I'll explain what I've made and you can taste them all, then decide if you want one in particular, a combination with three separate tiers or something else entirely,' Riya explains.

'Wonderful.' Ava nods.

Joe climbs onto his dad's lap while they taste the cakes and shares his opinions, too. With his fine blond hair and big brown eyes, he's very cute. Ava and Edward involve him in their decision making and I can see how happy this makes him. When he asks for a special cake for his dog too, Edward stiffens slightly while Ava laughs, but Riya, ever the professional, tells Joe she can definitely make a cake for his dog and that she's done so before. Riya is amazing and in the café, she has a section of the cake fridge reserved for dog treats she makes — all grain and additive free. They also stock doggy ice cream because, as Maisie and Riya are fond of saying, why should dogs miss out?

When Ava and Edward have made their decision, Maisie makes us more coffees and we sit and chat.

'Are you having the traditional stag and hen parties?' Maisie asks as she sets a tray of drinks down on the table.

Ava glances at Edward and he smiles at her, then shakes his head. 'It took me long enough to find this woman, so the last thing I want is to spend time away from her deliberately. If anything, we'd like to have a joint party. Do you have any suggestions, Grace?'

I blink, momentarily frozen as images of Bear flash through my mind. Something about Edward's confidence and charisma reminds me of the man I spent last night with. A pang of longing for him surprises me. I knew it was a one-night thing, that I'd never see him again, and yet it seems that part of me wishes that wasn't true.

'I do, actually. I've had other clients who prefer to do a joint thing. How about booking a restaurant and then heading to a club for some dancing? Or you could hire a venue and just have a big party.'

'What do you think, Ava?' Edward asks.

She nibbles at her bottom lip. 'I don't mind.'

'Ava ...' Edward laughs. 'It's fine for you to be honest.'

'I like the restaurant idea.' She smiles at him.

'Restaurant followed by a club, it is then,' Edward says. 'Can I leave the details to you, Grace?'

'Of course.' I nod, already flicking through my mental Filofax as I try to think what restaurants will be available for a large group at short notice. I have a few ideas already.

'Can I come, Daddy?' Joe asks.

Edward laughs. 'Not to that one because it's just grownups, but you'll definitely be at the wedding and the party afterwards.'

'Hooray!' Joe giggles. 'I can't wait for Kismet to have her cake.'

'It'll be the highlight of the wedding day, I'm sure.' Edward winks at Ava over Joe's head and I see a glance pass between them that makes my heart flutter. They are so in love and it makes me feel ... lonely. I'm happy for them, but I wish I had what they have too. I thought I did once, but it turned out I was mistaken and then ... last night ... there was so much about Bear that I liked and he's the kind of man I could grow to care about. Giving myself a mental shake, I push the thoughts away. What's the point? It was clear that it wasn't going anywhere other than the bedroom, and for one night only. Even if there was the possibility of more, I wouldn't want it because I've been hurt before and I don't want to be hurt again. Not ever.

I grab my laptop from the next table and we run through some more details then I give them feedback on the flowers and caterers. Everything is coming together nicely and I'm pleased that they trust me to do this for them.

After they've gone, it's time to tidy up. I'm tired and looking forward to soaking in a bath and then having an early night. I hope my dreams won't be filled with replays of my night with Bear, although I have no idea how to prevent it because my body still thrums with the memory of his touch.

# Chapter 13

## *Jack*

'Hi Mum.' I raise a hand in greeting as my mother's familiar face appears on the screen in the lounge.

'Hello darling.' She smiles and I notice the pink lipstick on her teeth that I know she'd be mortified about. 'How are you?'

'Good, thanks.'

She leans forwards. 'You look tired. I hope you're not working too hard.'

'I'm always working too hard,' I reply with a laugh.

'All work and no play makes Jack a dull boy.' She flashes me a wink and I laugh again, but this time wryly. I know where this is going and I wish it wasn't.

'I'm fine, Mum, and there's nothing dull about me, I promise you.'

My mother pushes her grey hair behind her ears and adjusts her gold heart locket. I know that inside that locket is a tiny photo of me with my two younger brothers, Will and Henry, taken when we were children. Will is two years younger than me at thirty-two and Henry is thirty. My mother always wears the locket and often toys with it when she's worried about one of us. We grew up in York where my parents still live but my brothers and I live in London now, much to Mum's chagrin. 'Darling, you're my eldest boy and I worry about you. All I want is for you to be happy and cared for. Living and working in London as you do ... you need someone there to look after you.'

'I do just fine, Mum.' An image from last night flashes through my head and I try to push it away because that is not the sort of thing I want to picture while I'm speaking to my mother. But last night ... Goldie did take good care of me as I hope I did of her. It hits me then that I wish I had her number, that I'd arranged to see her again, even asked for her real name. I didn't because I thought it was for the best. *It is for the best, for fuck's sake, Jack.* The last thing I need is to get involved with someone because it can never ever go anywhere. I have to stay single and cannot offer anyone commitment ever again.

'What is that?' she asks.

'What?'

'You look ... strange. Like there's something on your mind.'

'Oh ... sorry, I was thinking about a meeting I have in the morning,' I lie. 'It's an important one with a supplier and I just remembered something I need to do before it.' Few things dominate my thoughts other than work, but it seems that Goldilocks is the exception. This is madness. She's probably nothing like she seemed last night, and it was just an act she put on to please me and herself.

'So ...' My mother licks her lips and I brace myself. *Here we go ...* 'I saw an old friend yesterday.'

'Oh?' I raise my eyebrows and breathe in slowly, but my jaw clenches automatically and my teeth press together so hard my right eye twitches. Stress really isn't good for you.

'Yes, darling. I bumped into Verity Copthorne at the nail salon and ... well ... she was looking good, although I suspect she's had some nips and tweaks here and there, probably a touch of Botox, you know.' Her hands go to her face and she touches the corners of her eyes, then her forehead as if to try out said cosmetic treatments. 'Anyway ... She asked about you.'

'Did she?' My voice is as flat as I suddenly feel. I don't want to talk about Verity Copthorne, nor do I want to even think about her.

'She's still very sad about what happened. She said you and Lara were good together and your old friend... the one Lara took up with... well between you and me, it doesn't sound like he's treating her very well.'

My jaw is clenched so hard now I'm worried I'll crack a tooth. As angry as I still am at Lara for what she did, I can't stand the thought of anyone treating her badly. Call it a fragment of shrapnel remaining from our old connection or misplaced loyalty on my part, but fuck it, I still care about her and always will do in some way. You don't grow up with a woman and stop caring about her as soon as she walks out of your life.

'I see,' I say, but my mouth is dry and I'm struggling to swallow, so I get up and go to the sideboard and pour myself a bourbon. Taking a swig, I return to the sofa and sit back down, glass cradled between my hands.

'I was thinking, Jack, that maybe if you spoke to Lara ... you could ... find a way through things?'

The hope in my mother's eyes cracks a new crevice in my already damaged heart. She cared about Lara and saw her as the daughter she'd never I had. I know she did, and for that same reason, I could not tell her the truth about what Lara did. Instead, I let her think we'd disagreed over when we planned to start a family because of my work commitments and we were unable to find a way through it. I knew if I told Mum what Lara had done, then it would have broken her heart and made her question the trust she'd put in the young woman she'd known since she was a child. I didn't want to do that to Mum, she's been through enough. She also has this mistaken belief that if all her sons are married off, then we'll be fine for the rest of our lives and her job will be done. I swear having cancer did this to her because she now worries about what will happen to us when she's gone. Although she has been given the all clear, the impact of cancer remains with someone even after treatment ceases. I've seen it with my own eyes with Mum and she'll never be the same person she was before the diagnosis. She's strong as fuck, a total warrior queen, but there's something in her eyes these days, an acceptance of her mortality that wasn't there before. She's been to the edge and seen what's there and she knows it could happen again, so it's like she's constantly preparing for that. Despite everything though, her family is her priority and making sure her husband and three sons all have a plan in place should anything happen to her. Not that she's not living her life, because she is with aplomb, but she's also ... aware. Yes, that's it, she's aware that she needs to be ready and that her family does too. God, I love the woman so much and would give her the moon on a stick if I could.

'Mum,' I say gently, 'Lara and I can't go back to how things were. That was a long time ago now and we've both changed. Besides which, it sounds like she's still with ... with him.' I know his name as well as I know my own, but I don't want to let it cross my lips. What happened made me feel like a failure because if I'd been what Lara needed, then she'd never have done what she did. The memory of what I saw still makes my stomach churn. But it's in the past now and I've moved on — because I had to. There will be no going back. I have the tattoos to prove it.

'Well according to Verity, she doesn't think it will last much longer so there's hope for you yet, darling.' Mum's earnest smile makes my heart ache and so I nod dutifully. 'I only wish you'd consider reuniting with Lara because since you split up, what was it ... four or five years ... ago, you've been alone. At least as far as I know, anyway, and so I wondered if it's because you still love her and can't get over her.' Her fingers stray to the locket again and she turns it over and touches the inscription on the back: *A mother's love never wavers ...*

'Any other news?' I ask, keen to get her to move on and thankfully she does, talking about my father and brothers. I know that my father, brothers and I are her entire world and I never cease to be amazed by her devotion to her family. She's an incredible woman and I'm so grateful to have her as my mum.

When she ends the call, I sit for a while on the buttery soft leather sofa where last night I held Goldie in my arms, intent on being in the moment and not worrying about what came next. We should live life like that really because we never know what's around the corner. And yet ... there's a hole inside me that nothing can fill — not work, drink, sex ... nothing. I try to live in the moment, but occasionally, especially in the lonely hours of the night, I wish I had someone to share it with.

## Chapter 14

## *Grace*

Through one of my contacts I was able to book a place in Queen's Park that boasts not only a ground-floor restaurant but also a loft where groups can hold private parties. I arrive at three-thirty, deliberately early so I can check everything is in place for Ava, Edward, and their guests. It's so sweet that they're keen to have this party together and I can't deny that it has made me think about how I spent a similar night. Being aware of what can happen on stag weekends — it's hard to completely avoid social media posts and the 'in jokes' from grooms and their friends afterwards — I had concerns that there would be strippers, possibly prostitutes and at the very least, a lot of alcohol consumed. Perhaps if I had felt more loved, secure, and that I had nothing to doubt him for, then I wouldn't have been so churned up but as it was, my ex had form and I knew he would probably get up to no good. They say that you should feel secure in yourself and love yourself so that if the person you're with ever hurts you, then you can walk away without too much damage. Or something like that anyway. But I devoted a lot of time to loving him and looking out for him and being who he wanted me to be, and it consumed a lot of energy. It's why I never want to place myself in that situation ever again. I don't want to lose myself or ruin how far I've come by surrendering parts of my heart and soul to a man who will never love me the way I'd like to be loved.

When you look at the venue from outside on the street, it seems like two separate mews houses, but once you step inside, it becomes evident that they have been joined together. The space is light, airy and elegant and I'm glad I chose it because it's perfect for Ava and Edward. The manager greets me then takes me in a lift to the loft, where I smile as I look around. Natural light streams through floor to ceiling windows and skylights, clean white floors and walls make it seem even bigger and the air is cool, laced with aromas of citrus and spice. They have laid tables in a rectangle so that the fifty guests can see everyone present, and it's ideal for speeches and toasts. Bottles of champagne sit in ice buckets ready for when people arrive, and I know from speaking to the manager when I booked the venue that staff will be ready and waiting to cater to the guests' needs.

'Let me know if there's anything else I can do,' the manager — a woman named Gwenllian, with cropped white hair, green framed glasses and lively grey eyes — says to me with a warm smile.

'I will do, thank you.'

She goes downstairs in the lift while I meticulously inspect the loft, ensuring perfection in every detail. I pride myself on ensuring that everything is perfect for my clients and while I know it would be good to delegate certain jobs to an assistant, I'm still at the stage where I prefer to be in control of everything. After all, it's my reputation at stake and my business, and while it's still growing, I can't take any risks. I've even recruited Maisie and Riya occasionally, because who else could I trust more than my beloved family? Of course, I know that as the business continues to grow, then I'll need to employ a team, but that's all ahead of me and so for now I'll continue to check everything myself. Quality assurance by Grace...

Laughing to myself, I cross to the windows and look down at the street. A limousine pulls up and then another and my stomach flutters because this is it, the event is about to begin. Something about a figure exiting the second limousine makes me lean closer to the glass, but then I shake my head. Most people will look similar from this distance and it couldn't possibly be him now could it? I'm probably just super sensitive, looking for him in places he wouldn't be because part of me wants to see him again. The sensitive area between my legs has no common sense at all and it's like it's woken up after a lengthy sleep and now it wants more growly Bear...

I take my bag containing my laptop, iPad, and other belongings over to the discreet bar in the far corner of the room and place it on the surface, then find my compact. After patting some translucent powder over my face, I apply some lipstick and check my hair to ensure my neat chignon is still in place. The black bodycon dress, tuxedo style blazer and stiletto heels are smart enough for a restaurant, yet when I remove the blazer, I'm club ready. I love black clothes because of their adaptability and because they're slimming. Although ... a shiver of delight runs down my spine as I think of how Bear reacted to my curves, how he made me feel when he looked at me with such hunger in his eyes and how he touched me like he'd never seen anything so delectable. No man has ever looked at me in that way before and I suspect no man ever will do again. I'm just not one of those women that men admire in that way.

I slip my bag behind the bar and take a deep breath, then head over to the doors to the lift and wait for Ava and Edward to arrive.

# Chapter 15

## *Jack*

I've brought a date. Talia *something*. Jones or James or ... I'm uncertain and it doesn't matter, anyway. I thought I should make an effort to bring a date, but I barely know this woman. She's a friend of a friend, so this is kind of more like a blind date, and while she's pretty ... she's not really my type. She's tall and slim and she has shiny red hair that tumbles down her back in waves that I suspect were created with overnight rollers. (I know these things because I've seen women get ready to go out and I do listen when female acquaintances talk to one another about how they got their hair and makeup a certain way. You never know when such information might be useful, so I absorb everything I can. Plus, I find women fascinating and like to understand them.) Talia smells like pomegranates and pink pepper and has a wide smile that exposes perfectly white and straight teeth. In fact, as we travel up in the lift, I realise she reminds me a bit of a young Julia Roberts in *Pretty Woman*, all nervous glances and doe eyes, but whereas Julia Roberts seemed genuinely nervous and sweet, this woman seems ... like she's putting it all on a bit.

For me? Possibly. Who knows? Perhaps it's her thing to act this way or perhaps my radar is off and I've misread her and she is like this all the time. Anyway, as I watch her, I feel nothing. Not even a desire to see if the breasts defying gravity in her strapless blue dress are fake or if she's a real redhead. *Wow!* What is wrong with me? By now, I'd usually be planning what would happen later on at the club and then when I get her home, but I don't want to take her to the club or home for that matter. Stifling a yawn, I hold out a hand as the lift opens, and she enters the loft in front of me.

We accept the flutes of champagne that are offered to us, then we walk into the space and I look around. It's nice, very nice in fact, and when I see Edward and Ava across the room, I catch his eye and he waves me over.

'Do you want to come and say hello?' I ask my date.

'Oh ... I'd like to use the ladies' first,' she says, flashing me that wide smile with slightly shaky lips and a flick of her hair, then handing me her glass.

I nod and she walks away, swaying her slim hips as if hoping I'm watching her. Sighing, I look away and then walk over to Edward, regret filling me. I should have come here alone and not felt the need to bring a date. At least then I could've relaxed. Instead, I'm already on edge because I'll have to entertain this woman when all I want is to talk to my friends and help Edward celebrate his good fortune in finding a woman to love and adore.

When I reach Edward, he pats my upper arm and Ava kisses my cheeks. I feel some of the tension inside me ebb away. Until, that is, a figure behind Edward turns around.

Suddenly, I am gazing into hauntingly beautiful eyes I thought I'd never see again.

'What are you doing here, Goldilocks?' I ask before I can stop myself.

Her eyes widen, her jaw drops and I see she's just as shocked to see me.

'Jack, meet Grace, our wedding planner. Grace, this is Jack, one of my best friends.' Edward grins at us both as if he hasn't a care in the world. I find myself grinning too, but suspect I look more like a ventriloquist's dummy than a man who's pleased to meet a stunning woman for the first time.

# Chapter 16

## *Grace*

Realising that I'm gaping at Bear, who I now know is called Jack, I force my mouth closed and swallow hard. After I've taken a deep breath, I lick my lips then say, 'Hello, Jack.' It has been just a week since we spent the night together but I've thought about him every single day.

'Hello, Grace,' he replies, and after passing one flute of champagne he's holding to Edward, he holds out his hand.

I take it and a bolt of electricity shoots up my arm. His pupils dilate as if he's felt it too, and he tugs gently, pulling me forwards. He leans towards me and kisses my left cheek, his breath warm on my skin, his beard tickling, then he does the same on the other side and I almost swoon. My whole body responds to his proximity and then he whispers in my ear, 'You look sensational.'

When he releases my hand, I wobble on my heels and have to fight to steady myself. What is it with this man? Why is my reaction to him so visceral? So ... unprecedented?

'If I didn't know better, I'd think you two already know each other,' Ava says, looking between us with a curious smile on her lips.

'London is a lot smaller than we think,' Jack says with a laugh. 'We've probably been in the same place on many occasions and move in similar circles. After all, it's not the first wedding I've ever been to, so it's highly likely that Grace has planned a wedding I've attended at some point.'

'Highly likely,' I say through gritted teeth, although I'm sure I never saw him at one of the weddings I've planned. There's no way I'd have forgotten his handsome face and seductive eyes, the way he looks at me like I'm the only other person in the room. Fuck no, I wouldn't have forgotten that for a second.

'But you just called Grace *Goldilocks,*' Ava says with a small frown. 'That's not really appropriate if you've just met, Jack.' She's smiling now as if she's teasing him, but I know what she means. It would be quite forwards of him.

'I uhhh ... Grace does seem familiar, but it's possible I've got her mixed up with someone else,' Jack replies with a grin.

'Got who mixed up?' A tall redhead appears at his side and places a hand possessively on his arm with a pointed glance at me. It makes me want to ask her what she thinks I'm doing here. It's so annoying when women like her see every other woman as competition.

'Hello you.' Jack slides an arm around her waist and she steps closer to him, flicks her long red hair over her shoulders and flutters her eyelashes.

'Right, are you ready to take your seats?' I look at Ava and Edward, keen to get out of the way of Red's radar before she shoots me down.

'Absolutely!' Edward takes Ava's hand. 'The sooner we eat, the sooner I can take my fiancée dancing and show off my best disco moves.'

'Oh god,' Ava says, rolling her eyes. 'Look out, everyone!'

As they walk away, Jack catches my eye and winks, but I turn on my heel and head for the bar to get my iPad. I need to distract myself, to immerse myself in my work, because that is why I'm here. It's quite clear that Bear has gone and Jack has come in his place and brought with him a replacement for Goldilocks. I have only myself to blame for allowing any feelings to rise inside of me when I saw him. We were both very clear about that fact that we wanted nothing other than one night of passion when we were together, and that is how it should stay. Jack's date is beautiful, elegant and sophisticated and clearly adores him. I am here to work and that is what I will do. This is my business and my business is my world now. I won't ever let anything, not even animal magnetism, get in the way of that.

THE DINNER at the loft went well and Edward, Ava and some very merry guests then filtered off to the next venue. I sorted everything with the manager of the restaurant then followed in an Uber, even though Ava had said they would wait for me in the limo. I wanted to maintain some distance between me and them because, while they are lovely, they are my clients. Ava, though, treats me like I'm a dear friend and it's strange because I find myself believing that I might actually become her friend after their wedding is done.

The club is the complete opposite of the restaurant, with its dark walls, low lighting, and loud music. We have the VIP area on the top floor of three, and when I arrive, I see that the party is in full swing. It makes me smile because everything is going to plan.

I cross the VIP area, feeling the thud of the base reverberating in my chest, and go to Ava and Edward. They smile up at me from what looks like a very comfortable leather couch. Ava pats the seat next to her and so I sit down and she takes my hand, then leans closer.

'Thank you so much for arranging all this for us,' she says into my ear because the music is loud. 'I know you're a wedding planner and that this could be outside of your remit, but we both trust you to achieve what we'd struggle to do ourselves.'

'It's a pleasure,' I say with a nod. 'I have plenty of contacts and so it was no problem at all to do this too.'

'You know so many people.' I notice her eyes are shining and I'm not sure if it's from emotion, champagne, or a combination of both.

With a small shrug, I say, 'I've developed a lot of contacts over the years and it works well for me and for them.'

'I really admire you for what you do, Grace.'

'Thank you. I admire you too, Ava.'

'Me?' Her eyebrows raise slowly.

'Yes. You are kind, sweet and courageous, Ava. I've only known you a short time, but what I've seen of you shows me that Edward is fortunate to have you. After all, you're marrying a single dad with a young son. That's brave, in my opinion.'

She smiles. 'I love them both so much. It's not brave. It's amazing how lucky I feel.'

'They are lucky too.'

She turns in her seat and runs the back of her free hand over Edward's cheek. He leans closer and kisses her tenderly. When she whispers something in his ear, he nods, then she turns back to me. 'Come on, then.'

'Come on, what?'

Standing, she takes my hand and pulls me up. 'Time to dance.'

'Oh ... But I ... I ...'

'No excuses, Grace. I want to dance with you.'

We head for the dance floor together and I find that I'm giggling. Yes, this is work but everything is running smoothly, Ava and Edward are happy and I guess I can let my hair down now. Besides which, Ava is paying me for this evening and if she wants me to dance, then that's what I'm going to do.

When we get to the middle of the dance floor, Ava holds my arms for a minute then leans forwards. 'Don't tell anyone, but I'm a bit tipsy,' she says to me. 'I've had such a wonderful evening and all the champagne has gone to my head.'

'I'm glad to hear that you've had a good time.'

'I'm just so happy, Grace. So so happy.'

The song ends and a temporary quiet falls over the club, but then the familiar opening beats of a song begin and Ava's eyes light up.

'OMG I love this song! I'm crazy in love too!' She claps her hands, then turns around and starts shaking her behind.

As Beyonce's gorgeous voice fills the club, I move my body too, and soon we're shaking everything we've got and laughing together as we sing the lyrics. I'd forgotten how much I enjoy dancing and so I let go, allow the music to guide me and sing my heart out to the familiar song.

## Chapter 17

## *Jack*

Talia tried to get me to dance, but I politely declined so she headed for the dance floor with a few other women. It's not that I hate dancing, I just don't feel in the mood. Not to dance with her, anyway.

Grabbing another drink from the bar, I return to the VIP area and look around. Where is Goldie, AKA Grace, now? I notice Edward is sitting with two other men, probably talking business even though he swore he wouldn't do that tonight, and Ava is not with him. My eyes slide across to the dance floor and there, through the bodies moving in time to a song my brain registers as Beyonce, I spy her. It's like the crowd parts and a spotlight appears on her because I can see her so vividly.

Grace is magnificent. In that tight black dress, her every curve is accentuated as if the dress was custom made. The heels elongate her legs and give her movements extra sway and I swear blood rushes to my groin as I gaze at her as if hypnotised.

I want her.

I can't deny it. I know how good it feels to run my hands over those curves, to kiss her pretty lips and to thrust my cock into her tight, wet warmth, to feel her clench around me as she comes.

She's laughing as she dances with Ava, and I find myself smiling too. She's a good dancer, moves in time with the music and shakes those full hips in a way that could drive a grown mad wild. It hits me then that I don't know much at all about her. She's a stranger, an enigma, and yet she's not. She's someone I've been intimate with. I've been intimate with lots of women, but with her, it was different. I can't pinpoint why right now but I know that I want to hold her again. This is dangerous, unchartered territory for me. I made a vow to myself to never spend more than one night with a woman, and yet, as I down my drink and place the glass on a nearby table, I don't care.

Tonight, I need to hold Grace again. I am fast becoming obsessed with her.

Before I can reason with myself, I'm crossing the floor and heading right towards her.

# Chapter 18

## *Grace*

Beyonce changes to Sugababes, and Ava claps her hands as we dance around each other. I'm having so much fun and am lost in the music when I feel a hand on my arm and another on my waist. I turn to meet unfamiliar eyes.

'Hey there, sexy, I've been watching you and I couldn't look away.'

The man's breath stinks of beer and cigarettes, and there's something in his eyes that scares me. He grabs my chin and lowers his head towards mine, his eyes fixed on my mouth, and I freeze. I'm paralysed with fear as a voice in my mind screams at me to move, but his grip is unyielding. Nausea rises in my throat and ice runs in my veins.

Suddenly, his head bounces to one side as a fist meets his cheek. His grip on me loosens, and he falls to the floor like a stone in a pond. Something crosses his face and he goes to get up, but another punch lands on him from above.

Screams and shouts pierce the air between the beats of the song and then I realise what's happening.

'Jack, no!' I scream as I reach for him and grab at his hand before he can punch the man again. He turns to me and there's something in his eyes that's wild and primitive and it makes my heart pound. But I shake my head, touch his chest, and place my hand over his heart. It's racing like mine and I hold his gaze, needing him to know that I'm OK.

'Please don't!' I shout to be heard above the music. I'm aware of people around us: bouncers grabbing the man on the floor and dragging him away, Edward with his arms around Ava, other people surrounding us in a protective circle as if to stop anyone seeing us in this moment of raw vulnerability.

I wrap an arm around Jack's waist and we walk through the crowd of Edward and Ava's guests and over to the VIP area. We sit in a corner booth behind a pillar and I turn so I can see him better. He's trembling, and it makes my heart ache to see him like this.

'What was that?' I ask, my vision blurring at the shock on his face. 'Are you OK?'

He stares into space for a few moments that feel like years and then he says, 'I watched him come for you and I ... I saw red. He put his hands on you and I was worried he'd hurt you. I couldn't let that happen.'

'I'm OK.'

'You froze.' His eyes bore into mine, but there's no anger in them now, just bewilderment.

'I did, I know. I was shocked. Ava and I were having fun and then that man came out of nowhere.'

Edward appears in front if us and crouches down. 'You both all right?' he asks.

We nod, and he places a hand on Jack's knee. 'He's gone now. They've kicked him out of the club.'

'Will Jack be in trouble?' I ask, fear like an icy hand around my throat.

Edward shakes his head. 'It's sorted.'

I see the glance that passes between the two friends and understanding dawns upon me. These men have money and money opens doors and closes them on things you need hidden. They don't need to worry about this because everyone will have seen the stranger grab me and Jack come to my aid.

No man has ever come to my aid like that before. He cared enough to come to my rescue and to actually hit that man. Not that I'm condoning violence because I really don't, but Jack acted on instinct and he set out to protect me. The knowledge does something funny to my insides and I feel wobbly, like I might be coming down with a fever. Jack came to my rescue – again.

'I'd better check on everyone,' I say, making to stand, but Edward shakes his head.

'It's fine, Grace. It's all fine. Stay here with Jack and have a drink.'

Nodding, I sit back and sigh, stretch my legs out in front of me, and try to let the tension flow from me.

'Sorry. I should say sorry,' Jack says. 'It wasn't appropriate for me to react like that. I'm no thug, I promise, but I didn't want him touching you.'

'It's OK.' I take his hand between both of mine. 'I'm grateful.'

'For what?'

'No one has ever stuck up for me like that before. Well, except for my aunt, and she never actually hit anyone.'

'No?' His eyes scan my face and I feel a blush rise to my cheeks at the intensity of his gaze.

'She can be fiery and she's always been in my corner, but with things like teachers who kept me in detention for doing things I hadn't done and, well ... you know, things like that. But she never hit any of them.'

*She did speak sternly to the parents of bullies who put chewing gum in my hair and all over my school blazer, so I had to have my hair cut and buy a new blazer.* I don't add the last bit, the shame of it still too raw, even after fifteen years. Why is there always shame in being bullied, as if we bring it upon ourselves? As if there's something embarrassing about being picked on for not fitting in with everyone else. It's not the way things should be, I'm sure, but it is the way things are. Even as a rational adult, I can still feel the burn of that childhood shame when bullies made me feel like I wasn't good enough to be their friend and so they chose to persecute me instead.

'No one ever has the right to make you feel less than wonderful, Grace,' he says. 'Because you are wonderful.'

He leans towards me, his eyes on my lips and my breath catches in my throat. *Is he going to kiss me? Here? Now?*

'Jack!' I see blue heels and long legs, a blue dress. Looking up, I see Jack's date towering over us, hands on hips, her face dark with fury. 'What happened?'

I glance at Jack, then back at her and know I must concede defeat. I stand then step aside, watching as the woman slips into my seat as if it belongs to her. As if Jack belongs to her. Perhaps he does.

'Excuse me,' I say, and I hurry away.

My vision blurs and I tell myself it's because I'm tired and wrung out but my heart screams that it's because Jack is possibly the most amazing man I've ever met and he's with someone else. Whatever it was that I thought was blossoming between us just then, I was wrong. Very wrong. What I thought was a special moment, was nothing of the sort and Jack is already taken.

I wipe the tears away with the back of my hand and stride towards the toilets, intending on washing my face, tidying my makeup and assuming my professional air once again.

After all, I have a job to do. I am not here to find love.

# Chapter 19

## *Grace*

Two days later, I'm sitting at a small table in the corner of my aunt's café. I'm meant to be working but my concentration is shot and I keep gazing out of the window at the beautiful spring day. Monday comes around so quickly and I can't believe it's the start of a new week.

A new week when I am single.

A new week when I'll try not to think about what happened on Saturday night, when Jack defended my honour like some chivalrous knight in a fairy tale.

A new week when I have to accept that Jack probably went home with another woman while I came home alone.

And that's fine. I enjoy being single. Most of the time, anyway. I have lots to do and need to stop moping around like some soppy teenager fantasising about the high school heart throb she can never have.

My eyes are drawn to the world outside the window again where a tree is heavy with pink blossom the colour of candy floss. As I watch, the breeze gently shakes the branches and blossom falls like confetti to the paved ground. It reminds me I need to check up on the order for biodegradable confetti. Ava requested dried flowers, which are a favourite with brides this year.

I add a note to my phone, then look up again and spot a fat grey pigeon waddling through the blossom, bobbing his head as he searches for food. Another pigeon joins him and then a courtship dance begins with the first pigeon chasing the second one around the tree. It's a comical scene and makes me think that love can be quite comical at times, with all the stressing we do over things that really shouldn't matter. Love should be more straightforward, but sadly, human beings are complicated creatures, and no relationship comes with an instruction manual or a guarantee.

An hour later, I've made some phone calls and chased up some emails and I'm sipping a frothy latte when the door opens, making the small brass bell tinkle. I look up instinctively, smiling as I prepare to greet one of the regulars, but my breath catches in my throat.

'Hi!' Jack smiles at me. In an exquisite navy suit with a crisp white shirt and navy tie, he looks edible.

'Hello.' I push my chair back, preparing to stand, but he comes over to the table so I stay put. What's he doing here? 'Aren't you working?' I ask. It is Monday, after all.

'I have been at the office but I needed to pop out for a bit.'

'Oh ... What for?'

'To get you these.' He places a gift bag on the table. 'To apologise again for what happened on Saturday.'

'Oh ... There's no need.' I stand now, straightening my purple blouse over my black trousers. I wish I was wearing something a bit nicer, but I didn't think I'd be seeing anyone of any import this morning.

'There is a need.' He reaches into the gift bag and pulls out a bouquet of red tulips. 'I'm sorry for behaving like a caveman on Saturday. Can you forgive me?'

With a smile, I accept the tulips and reply, 'Of course I can, but as I mentioned, there's no need for an apology. I was a bit taken aback, but not in a bad way. I mean ... obviously I don't condone violence but that man ... well ... he was out of line and ...' I look up from the flowers and see that Jack is smiling.

'He was out of line and while I'm sorry for hitting him in front of you like that, I still feel that he needed to be put in his place. But still ... I should have dealt with it better. I just saw red.'

How can I be so torn between being aware that violence is not the answer and incredibly flattered that he hit the creep to protect me? He saw red because that man was sleazing on me. I'm so confused right now, and it makes me wonder what's going on here.

'No one has ever hit someone to protect me before,' I say, then lower my gaze to the beautiful flowers again. 'These are lovely, thank you.'

'There's a box of chocolates in the bag too.' He pushes it

towards me, and I peer inside it and see what looks like a luxury box of Belgian truffles.

'Thanks. Although I probably shouldn't eat them.'

'What? Why ever not?' A frown mars his otherwise smooth brow.

'Well ...' I pat my stomach and heat rushes to my cheeks.

Jack leans over the table and holds my gaze. 'You are fucking gorgeous, Goldie, and don't you ever let anyone tell you otherwise.'

My heart does that fluttering thing it seems to do whenever he's around, and I take a shaky breath. My whole body tingles at the look in his eyes and I wish we were alone so I could move closer to him.

'Well, hello there.' Maisie has come over to the table and she looks at me expectantly.

'Umm ... Maisie this is Jack ...' Mortified, I realise I don't recall his surname.

'Jack Kendrick.' Jack holds out his hand and Maisie shakes it.

'This is my aunt, Maisie Cosgrove.'

'Very pleased to meet you,' she says as she shakes his hand. 'And how do you know Grace?'

They both turn to me and my already warm cheeks blaze. How can I tell her that?

'We met through Edward and Ava,' Jack says, swooping in and rescuing me yet again. 'I'm one of Jack's best men.'

'I see.' Maisie nods and smiles, but I know from the way she looks at me, she's aware there's more to this. 'Can I get you a drink, Jack?'

'I'd love an Americano to go, thanks,' he says.

My heart sinks. He's not hanging around.

'Coming right up.' Maisie walks away and I sink back into my chair.

'I can see you're busy,' he says, 'so I don't want to disturb you.'

'You're not. I was due a break, anyway.' *Please stay for a bit.*

'Well ... in that case, I'll have my coffee here.' He pulls out a chair and sits opposite me. 'Great place, by the way.'

He looks around the café and I follow his gaze, taking in the décor I'm so familiar with. I see it the way he would do, from the blue woodwork to the reclaimed oak floorboards and the mix and match furniture that Maisie and Riya bought from a local antiques dealer on Portobello Road. They had the cushions for the chairs made from old blankets and clothing, and up-cycled some of the furniture themselves, like the sideboard that holds the cutlery and napkins, painting everything in a rainbow of colours. The café is pretty, cosy and so wonderfully uniquely them.

'It's lovely, right?'

'Do you work in here often?' he asks.

'I do,' I reply, being deliberately vague. At the moment, I'd prefer not to discuss my reasons for working here. 'I find it helps me to be surrounded by people, plus it's an excellent spot to meet up with clients.'

*Healing the Billionaire's Heart*

'Do you have an office around here someplace?' he asks and I swallow a sigh.

'Something like that.' Thankfully, Maisie arrives with his Americano and another latte for me, so we thank her and I close the lid of my laptop, knowing I won't get anything done while Jack's sitting with me.

We sit quietly for a few moments, and Jack sips his coffee. I can see Maisie and Riya glancing at us as they try to work out what's going on, and I know I'm going to be grilled later.

'How did you know where to find me?' I ask, realising that I never gave him my address.

'Ava,' he says. 'I told her I needed to ask your advice about my wedding speech. I hope that was OK?'

'Of course.'

'I wasn't sure you'd be here, but then I thought I could leave the flowers and chocolates for you. However, when I saw you sitting here ... well, it was like fortune smiled on me.'

His eyes are filled with mischief and I find it difficult to resist the urge to reach over the table and stroke his cheek.

'Do you have a busy week ahead?' I ask.

'Yeah meetings and the like ... a normal Cavendish Construction week, really, but I knew I wouldn't be able to focus until I'd apologised. It would have played on my mind.'

'Really?'

'Of course. You sound surprised.'

'Well, in my experience, men often don't care and can switch off from feelings to focus on work.'

'In my experience, so can some women.' He cocks an eyebrow at me and I smile.

'Touché.'

'Look Grace ... I've been ... living my life a certain way for some time. I won't bore you with the details, but something happened in my past and it left me ... hardened. And not in a good way, if you know what I mean.' He nods at his lap, and I laugh.

'Oh. Not that type of hard?'

'Exactly. And I haven't wanted to get to know any women. I mean, I sleep with women but as for anything else, well ... It's not what I want.'

Why is he telling me this? Have I seemed too keen, and he's telling me to back off?

'But you ... I don't know what it is, and I hope I don't regret telling you this but ... you're different.'

'Me?' My voice comes out as a squeak and I cough to clear my throat.

'Yes, you.'

'But what about Red?' I ask, needing to know even though I don't want to think about her.

'Red?' His brows meet.

'The woman you were with at the club.'

'Oh, her!' He laughs. 'Just a date for the evening. I barely knew her and have no intention of seeing her again.'

'I see.' My heart does a somersault and I bite the inside of my cheeks to stop myself grinning like an idiot.

'Look ... I'm not proposing here.' He laughs as if that is the funniest thing he's ever said. 'God, no, so please don't run screaming for the hills, but ... I would like to see you again. If you'd like that?'

His light brown eyes hold mine and I nod, feeling a rush of something that I can only describe as hope. But what am I hoping for here? I know my stance on dating and relationships, but the thought of never seeing this man again leaves me with an ache in my chest. The voice at the back of my mind is screaming, *Danger! Walk away now!* But I don't want to listen. I want to see him again.

'I'd like that.' I swallow. 'But I'm incredibly busy for the next few weeks with work. I don't know when ...'

His expression falters, then he seems to gather himself. 'I could help you with some of it. I'm quite skilled.'

He leans his elbows on the table, and I gaze at his strong hands. 'I know you are.' I flash what I hope is a sultry smile.

'So what do you think?'

'About what?'

'About me helping you? At least that way we can spend some time together.'

'I uhhh ... I have a wedding fayre on Wednesday evening.'

'Can I help you with that?'

'I-I guess so.'

'Brilliant. I'll be your assistant and can hand out fliers or direct people to your table or whatever else it is that you need me to do.' He pulls his phone from his jacket pocket. 'Give me your number and I'll send you mine.'

We're exchanging numbers now? This wasn't part of the original plan. But then he is just going to help me at the wedding fayre.

After he's added me to his contacts, I say, 'Are you sure? It's not beneath you with you being a high-flying business executive and all?'

'I enjoy seeing how things work and I'd like to see you, so I'm happy to help.'

'Great.' I don't know what else to say because I know that having Jack around will be a distraction and yet the thought of him being there is also uplifting. Plus, it means we'll be in a public place and there will be no opportunity for us to get intimate, and that's fine because I'm not sure my heart can take it right now. I'm too vulnerable after the amazing night we spent together and being intimate with him again might well make me fall for him, which I can never, ever allow myself to do.

He drains his coffee, then taps the cardboard cup on the table. 'I'll see you Wednesday then? You want me to pick you up?'

I think of the limo and what could happen in it and shake my head. 'I'll text you the address and meet you there.'

'Cool.' He stands up and takes his cup to the recycling bin, then says goodbye to Maisie and Riya before returning to my table. When he leans over and presses a kiss to my cheek, I am overwhelmed by his gorgeous scent, his cologne fresh and woodsy, his lips warm, his hand on my shoulder a reminder of the ecstasy of being touched by him. 'See you soon, Goldie.'

And then he is gone and I'm left sitting at the corner table, my thighs pressed together, my jaw tense. I do not know why he affects me so intensely, but I can't help wanting more. Jack Kendrick is hot as hell and I'm afraid I'm going to get hurt, but I can't fight these feelings. I don't want to fight them if I'm being honest with myself.

THAT EVENING, I'm curled up on the sofa with Maisie and Riya. I'm in my fleecy pjs with my hair piled on top of my head, my face scrubbed clean and moisturised. I have a spot coming at the side of my nose so I've rubbed toothpaste on it and I know I look a mess. None of this matters though because it's just my aunt and her partner here to see me like it. Maisie ordered Chinese takeaway, so I have a plate of egg fried rice, sweet and sour chicken balls and prawn toast and it's scrumptious.

So far, I've managed to evade interrogation, but I know that now that we're settled in front of the TV, they will consider me fair game.

'More wine?' Maisie holds up the bottle of Pinot Grigio.

'Go on then.' I hold out my glass and she pours wine into it then tops up hers and Riya's. I take a gulp because I know what's coming next.

'That man today ...' Maisie takes a sip of wine and waits for me to take the bait.

I don't. Instead, I drink again.

'The one in the expensive suit,' Maisie adds.

'Gorgeous man!' Riya nods. 'Even I could see that.'

'He was tasty, and he seemed to have eyes only for you,' Maisie says waving her fork at me.

'Stop waving cutlery at me.' I giggle, then stuff a chicken ball into my mouth.

'You're hiding something.' Maisie leans forwards on the sofa and frowns at me.

I look around their cosy lounge, taking in the patchwork throws over the sofas and chairs, the black and white photographs on the walls, the antique furniture that they both adore, and exhale slowly. This place is the only home I have now and I love it and yet I also know that me living with them can only be temporary. As much as I love them and they love me, I'm an adult and I can't stay here forever. For one thing, there's no privacy. Look at today and how I couldn't even speak to a handsome man without them wanting to know all the juicy details.

'I'm not hiding anything.' I shrug, but my damned cheeks flush.

'You're blushing.' Maisie puts her plate on the table and wipes her mouth with a napkin. 'Are you dating him?'

'Who?'

She rolls her eyes. 'Jack, of course.'

'Not dating exactly.' I sip my wine. 'But we have ... spent some time together.'

'I hope you're being careful, Grace,' Riya says, her expression serious. 'A man like that ... so handsome and clearly rich if the cut of his suit is anything to go by. Well, he could be dangerous.'

'I'll say!' Maisie pushes her hair behind her ears. 'Very dangerous.'

'I'm being careful.' Putting my plate on the table, I swallow a sigh. 'I barely know him and there's nothing going on, not really.'

'We love you, Grace, and don't want you getting hurt.' Maisie shakes her head. 'After what happened before ...'

'It's OK. I'm fine.' The urge to stomp out of the room and go to bed and cry rises inside me, but I'm a grown woman and not a teenager, so I stay put. Besides which, what good did having a tantrum ever really do? Better to face the music here and now.

Maisie drains her wineglass and sets it on the table, then she sighs. 'Grace, do you know what? You're only thirty. You're young and Riya and I worry about you being stuck at home with us two. At your age you should be enjoying yourself, dating and dancing and enjoying your freedom, but because of what happened, you barely do anything other than work.'

It's true, I know.

'Therefore, you should have some fun with this Jack. He's very charming and I'm sure he's fun to be with. As long as he treats you well, darling, enjoy yourself. You're only young once and the years fly.'

'That's so true.' Riya nods vigorously. 'It is possible to enjoy yourself and protect your heart.'

'I'm hardly going to fall in love with him,' I say, but there's a bitter taste on my tongue. They see Jack could end up hurting me and they're worried. I'm worried too and yet I don't want to not see him again. He's not my ex and while he's like him in that he's rich and successful and aware of how handsome he is — he must be because he has women falling over themselves to be with him judging by how that woman was at the hen and stag party — he's also his own person. I can't judge all men based on how I've been treated in the past. Besides which, it would be nice to enjoy some fantastic no strings sex.

'Finish your food,' Maisie says, gesturing at my plate. 'You need to keep your strength up.'

I shake my head. 'I'm full now, but thank you. It was delicious.'

Standing up, I grab my plate and glass and take them through to the kitchen. I scrape the plate off then put it in the dishwasher along with my glass. Maisie and Riya are right but I know that they're worried and I feel bad. I know it's because they've seen me hurt before and don't want to see it happen again but they're also right about having some fun.

When I turn, Maisie is standing in the doorway. She opens her arms and I step forwards and she hugs me tight. 'Sweet

Grace. Life is short and you must live it the way you want, but without fear or hesitation. I'm sorry. I let my own fear of seeing you get hurt again cloud my judgement, but you are young and you should be out having fun. Just because one man didn't see your worth, doesn't mean that all men are the same. It's not fair of me to suggest they are. Spend some time with Jack and see where it goes. You never know, he could be your person.'

I lean back and meet her gaze. 'I doubt that he's my person, but I do like him.'

'Then have fun with him.' She kisses my forehead then hugs me again and I send out a silent thank you to the universe for giving me such a wonderful aunt. I've lost a lot in my life, but Maisie has always been there and for that I am incredibly grateful.

## Chapter 20

## *Jack*

I've always loved my job and how I can immerse myself in work and not worry about a thing outside of it, but the past two weeks have been different. I'm distracted, and it's not good. Well, it is in some ways, but not as far as my commitment to work is concerned. It will pass, I hope, but for now I keep finding myself thinking of Grace. Dreaming of Grace. Longing to see her again.

Fuck, this isn't me! I'm in too deep for comfort. Perhaps I just need to get her out of my system and then I'll feel better. Yes, that's it. If I fuck her a few more times, the usual sense of boredom will set in and I'll be glad to say goodbye, to let her go so I can get back to normal ...

But I know that's not right. It's not how I operate and it's not how Grace deserves to be treated.

'What're you daydreaming about?' Edward has come into my office. He sinks onto the leather sofa near the window.

'Nothing.' Shaking my head, I get up and take the sofa

opposite him. 'I'm just a bit tired this morning.' Stifling a yawn, I rub my eyes.

'Late night?' Edward raises his eyebrows and I laugh.

'Not in that way. I was going through some emails and then I went to bed, but I couldn't drop off. When I finally passed out, I had some really vivid dreams. When I woke at dawn, I felt exhausted and like I hadn't slept at all.'

'Is everything OK?' There's concern in Edward's eyes. He knows me and he knows my past. 'Do you need to talk about anything?'

I groan and bury my face in my hands. 'I don't know.'

'What don't you know?' he prompts me.

'It's the ... the wedding planner.' I meet his gaze.

'Our wedding planner?'

'Yes.'

'Thought so.'

'You did?'

'Jack, you punched a guy in the face at the weekend for hitting on her.'

'He was being a creep.'

'Even so ... You don't normally go around punching guys for being creeps.'

'He was out of line.'

Edward's brows meet, and he rubs a hand over his mouth. 'I agree with you on that, but we can't go around punching every man we think is being a creep. We were lucky we were at a club where we could smooth things over with some cash and our reputation.'

'The manager said it was all caught on camera and that it went in my favour.'

He shrugs as if that's debatable. 'Even so ... You need to be careful, Jack. We're not at university now and have the company to think about.'

'Is this a warning?' I shift in my seat. This isn't like Edward. We're friends and we go back a long way. Fuck, I'm VP of operations. I don't get warnings.

'Jack, you're as good as a brother to me and it's because of that reason that I'm being honest with you. I am not warning you and never would. You know how things work. Reputation is important and we don't need you being labelled as pugnacious, or anything else for that matter.'

'I was protecting her honour and you'd have done the same for your fiancée.'

'I would have done the same for Ava,' he says, and I know he means it. 'But as you said, she's my fiancée. Grace is ... Well, I don't know what Grace is to you and it's not relevant, I guess, because no man should force himself on a woman and we should do what we can to prevent that. However, next time ... if there is a next time ... maybe get him outside the club first and away from the cameras. Just in case.' He winks and the tension I felt building dissipates.

'I'm not sure what's going on with me, to be honest. You know what I've been like since ... I don't get like this about women, but Grace is ... different.'

'She's also planning my wedding and I don't have time to find another wedding planner, plus Ava really likes her, so please don't break her heart before the wedding.'

'I have no intention of breaking anyone's heart.'

'Jack ... you have stayed well away from any commitment for some time now. While I appreciate you feel something's changing ... If you realise you don't like Grace enough to spend more time with her, then please take care. She's a lovely person, and I'd hate to see her broken-hearted when you say goodbye. Plus, it would make for a really awkward wedding day.'

'I won't hurt her.' I'm not even certain I'm being honest because how can I guarantee that I won't?

Edward nods. 'Well, in that case, see how it goes. Perhaps it will be different this time.'

'Perhaps.' I stare past Edward, out of the window and across London, wondering where Grace is right now and what she's doing. I realise I want to text her to find out, to check that she's OK.

'Are you seeing her again?'

'This evening.'

'That soon?' Edward raises his brows.

'Yeah ... but it's not a date. We're meeting up because she's attending a wedding fayre, and I said I'd give her a hand.'

'So you do like her then?'

Laughter bubbles up from my gut, and I incline my head. 'I think I do.'

'I can't wait to tell Ava.'

'What?'

'She told me she saw something in your eyes at the weekend, but I laughed it off. Now I have to let her know she was right.'

'In your eyes, she's always right.'

Edward smiles fondly as he rises and adjusts his tie. 'It's true, but what's a guy to do?'

As he leaves my office, I find myself agreeing wholeheartedly, *What is a guy to do?*

# Chapter 21

## *Grace*

The wedding fayre is at a venue at the Royal Docks in Newham, East London. It's a fantastic waterfront location, steeped in history and currently undergoing a fantastic revival. The fayre usually takes place over a weekend, but this is like a warm up evening where some smaller businesses will be featured before the big fayre in a few weeks' time. It was the idea of one of the cofounders who felt that while the big event works, it would be good to give some smaller business a chance too. I'm glad because this earlier event is for people like me.

I have my own booth at the fayre and I'm so excited. Yes, I had to pull a few strings to get it and yes, I'm nervous, but it's also a wonderful opportunity to get more business and to start growing things again. It's time now. I need to put the past behind me and to focus on the present and the future. Maisie and Riya dropped me off in their van and helped me to set up. They offered to stay and help but left after hearing that Jack was coming, reminding me to call if needed.

'Thought you might like this.' Jack appears as if out of thin air and he's holding a glass of champagne.

'Hello.' My heart somersaults at the sight of him. In a black shirt and trousers with his hair freshly cut and his beard neatly trimmed, he looks better than I remember. It's not fair that a man is this gorgeous, it's really not. I accept the champagne and take a sip. 'Thanks for this.'

'You're welcome.' He looks around. 'Fantastic venue!'

'I know, right?'

'Cavendish Construction is playing a major role in the regeneration of this site. It's exciting what's still to come.'

'Wow! I'd love to know more.'

'I can't say too much at the moment, but this area will continue to be developed over the next few years. I might even end up with my own place here.'

'You're building more luxury apartments?'

He winks at me. 'It's a perfect location, but we'll also be overseeing wildlife preservation, so there will be areas dedicated to that. As a company, we strive to ensure that while we create, we don't destroy. It's part of our ethos.'

'What exactly is your role in the company?' He mentioned something before, but I didn't quite understand it and felt too embarrassed to ask him to elaborate.

Jack leans on the counter of the booth and holds my gaze with his hypnotic eyes. 'I'm VP of Operations.'

'OK.' I sip my drink. I have no idea what that means but it sounds important.

'It means,' he says, as if reading my mind, 'That I have a hand in basically every department. I'm a Jack of all trades, to coin a phrase. Joking aside, though, I ensure all operations are profitable and perform in line with company expectations.'

'So you're ... like ... a supervisor?'

'Kind of. A very well paid one. And I have shares in the company, so it's in my interest as an employee and shareholder that the company continues to thrive.' He smiles. 'But it's a big role because I have to make sure that everything runs smoothly and that people are doing their jobs.'

'That's a lot of responsibility.' My admiration for him just keeps on growing. 'I only manage myself and sometimes that's hard enough.'

'I think you're amazing. I have people below and above me at work, but you're doing this all on your own. You're incredible, Grace.'

I know that he's being genuine as he says this and a tingle runs down my spine like a finger, sending goosebumps all over my skin.

'I think you're incredible,' I say.

'Excuse me.' A young couple have come to my booth so Jack steps aside and gestures for them to come closer. 'Could you tell us more about what you offer?' the woman asks.

'Of course,' I say. 'Come and have a seat.'

They walk through to the seating area and I glance at Jack, who takes my place at the counter. He really is going to help me this evening and I'm grateful. If it's busy, we won't get much time to talk, but I already feel that I've learnt more about him and who he is, about what he's capable of doing. A VP of operations for one of the biggest construction companies in the UK is helping me out at a wedding fayre. I can't see that ever sinking in because it's not exactly the sort of thing that happens every day, especially not to me.

Shaking myself inwardly in an attempt to focus, I put my musings about Jack to one side and focus instead on the couple in front of me. It's my time to shine.

# Chapter 22

## *Jack*

Watching Grace all evening, I have to admit that I'm impressed. There's something about her I really admire. She's calm and clear, warm and encouraging and an excellent salesperson. It was like she evaluated each couple that came to her booth and could predict what they were looking for and cater for their dream wedding. At this rate, she'll need to expand her company and it got me wondering why she works alone right now. Surely someone as enigmatic and impressive as she is should have employees. I'll ask her about that when I get a chance because this could be the perfect time for her to consider expanding her business. Perhaps I can even offer some advice. After all, I've got a few years of management under my belt.

I've also got something else under my belt and it's been twitching all evening every time I looked at her. Fuck, she's beautiful and I've been longing to have some time alone with her.

I help her load her things into her aunt's van and then pause as she turns to me.

'Thank you so much for your help this evening, Jack.'

'It was a pleasure. You impressed me and I enjoyed helping. Not that I did much, but...'

'You were wonderful.' She winces.

'What is it?'

'My feet are killing me.' She reaches down and adjusts one of her shoes.

'So ... are you going home now?' I ask, looking over at the van where her aunt is waiting and smiling.

Grace meets my eyes. 'Uhhh ... I wasn't sure.' Her smile makes my heart squeeze.

'Would you like to come back with me? I could make us some food.'

'I'd like that and I'm starving so food sounds really good.' She smiles. 'I'll just let Maisie know.'

While she's gone, I message my driver. I was planning on walking, but seeing her struggling after being on her feet so much this evening, it'll be better to take the limo.

'Maisie said to have fun.' Grace waves as her aunt drives away and then we're left alone. At last.

I slide my arm around her waist and pull her against me, stroke her hair back from her face. Desire flashes in her eyes when she feels how hard I am.

'I can't wait to get you home, Grace.'

Leaning forwards, I kiss her softly and a soft moan escapes from between her parted lips. There is nothing sexier than a woman who wants you. Who needs you. Who opens to you in every way. I want Grace to open herself to me and as the thought takes residence in my mind; I realise I don't just mean physically but in every way she can do: body, heart, and mind. I want all of her to belong to me. Even if it's just temporary.

IN THE LIFT UP to my apartment, we kiss tenderly, as if we have all the time in the world and are in no rush. I feel like a teenager again, desperate to do more yet holding back. I know what's coming, and it's even more delicious because I'm waiting for it. For Grace, I want to wait. Prolonging the event increases the anticipation.

Inside, we kick off our shoes and I take her hand, then lead her through to the lounge. She sinks onto the sofa and removes her jacket. I gaze at her, unable to remove my eyes from her white silk blouse. I can just about make out the lacy bra underneath it. When she stretches, the silk pulls taut against her breasts and it makes my cock grow even harder.

'Grace, you're killing me here.' I rub a hand over my length and she grins at me sexily.

'Show me,' she says.

*So much for waiting...*

'Hold on.' I go to the kitchen and get a bottle of champagne from the wine fridge, open it then grab two glasses. Realising I need to freshen up before I get started on her, I set the bottle and glasses on the counter and head for the bathroom. After a quick wash, I return to the kitchen and grab the champagne, then return to Grace.

I pause in front of the sofa and set the bottle and glasses down on the table gently because Grace is fast asleep. Her arms are above her head, her lips slightly parted and her skirt has risen up her thighs, exposing a tantalising flash of lacy black stocking tops. She is exhausted, and although I had thoughts about screwing her brains out this evening, I know she needs to rest.

I carefully scoop her up in my arms, then carry her through to the bedroom. Pushing the covers aside, I set her down on the bed, then tuck her in. When I press a kiss to her forehead, her eyes open a fraction.

'Jack?' She reaches for me.

'Get some sleep, precious Goldie,' I say before kissing her again.

'Thank you,' she whispers, then she falls straight to sleep.

I leave the room but don't close the door fully. If she needs me she can call for me and I'll be back like a shot. However, I have a feeling that Grace is out for the night. I'll catch up with some emails and grab a bite to eat, then slide in next to her and hold her close all night long. There's far more pleasure in that image than I'd expect, given that I rarely rest that well when a woman stays over.

## Chapter 23

## *Grace*

When I wake, I am aware of being warm and comfortable and wrapped in Jack's arms. The blinds are drawn but the bedroom door is open and the hallway is light. Closing my eyes again, I stay where I am for a few moments longer, not wanting to break the spell.

My eyes flutter open again when I feel Jack's lips feathering kisses over my nape and then my shoulders. He slowly moves his hands over me, pushing clothing aside so he can touch the skin of my stomach, my thighs, my back, and my breasts. He is spooning me and I feel his cock grow hard, pressing against the cheeks of my bottom.

'Morning,' I say and he growls into my shoulder then nips at my left earlobe.

'Morning, Goldie.'

He shifts position, so he's above me and he undoes my blouse all the way, pulls it over my arms, then unzips my skirt and slides it down my thighs. I lie before him in my lacy lingerie and stockings and he pauses as he gazes at me. His eyes are filled with hunger and I know he's about to devour me whole.

'I'm sorry I fell asleep last night,' I say, and he meets my eyes.

'You were exhausted after a busy and successful event.'

'How did I get in here?' I ask, realising I don't recall walking.

'I carried you.'

'You carried me? Did you hurt your back?'

'Cut it out!' He leans forwards and bites my bottom lip then teases his tongue around my lips. 'You are fucking gorgeous, Grace.'

'So are you.' I stroke his muscular thighs, run my hands up towards his groin and the enormous erection that's straining against his trunks. When I grip it through the material and rub my hands up and down the shaft, he closes his eyes and moans.

'That's my good Goldilocks.'

Slipping my hand through the flap in his trunks, I release his cock and touch the silky skin, rub my right thumb over the bead of pre-cum on the tip while fisting him with my left hand. He moves with me, fucking my hands, and I'm so turned on I could explode.

Suddenly, he stops my movements and pushes my hands above my head, then he slides my thighs apart with his knees, moves the lace of my panties aside and blows over my sex. The sensation is so delicate and yet tantalising and I wait for him to touch me there. Instead, he slides his hands under my bottom and lowers his head, then covers me with his mouth. He licks and sucks and nibbles, pushes his tongue inside me with small delicious flicks, and eats me until I'm at the brink. When he stops, I cry out with disappointment, and he grins up at me.

'Did I eat you good, baby?'

I pull him towards me by his cock until he's on top of me and then I grip his ass and rub against him until he slides inside. Holding him there, I savour the feeling of his width and his length, the pressure of him against my clit and labia, the coiled strength of his muscular body above me. I move my hips to take him deeper and his eyes widen, then he pulls out.

'Hold on.' He leans over and opens the drawer of the bedside cabinet and grabs a condom, tears the foil, then slides it on. 'I almost forgot, Grace. When I'm with you, it's too easy to forget to be sensible.'

I forgot too, but I want him so much I wouldn't have cared. He makes me lose all rational thought when we're together because my desire for him is so powerful.

He slides back inside me and we stay that way, gazing into each other's eyes until I can't take anymore, and I clench around him as I orgasm, stars shooting across my vision, my body bucking against him as I take him as deeply into me as I can.

He's smiling when I can focus again and he kisses me, tasting of me, smelling like me and it's so, so hot.

'I'm going to take you hard now, Grace, and I want you to scream my name.'

He grabs my legs and puts my ankles together over his left shoulder, then he turns me slightly so he's entering me at a deeper angle. His thrusts are slow at first but soon speed up and his cock hammers at my core, massages my g-spot at just the right angle and I come again, this time internally, and yes, I do scream his name as he shouts out mine.

Afterwards, he holds me against him, spooning me the way he did all night long. I am breathless, sated and yet yearning for more. I am elated and yet terrified, because I know I am falling for this man.

What am I going to do about it?

Perhaps if I sleep with him a few more times, I'll get bored and these irrational feelings will fade away ...

Who am I trying to fool?

## Chapter 24

### *Jack*

We shower together, and I soap Grace all over, savour the feel of her wet slippery curves as my hands slide all over them.

After we've dried off, I make us some scrambled eggs and crispy bacon, and we wash it down with strong black coffee. We eat at the kitchen island, stools close together and her feet rest on mine. There's something about being with Grace that helps me unwind. I'm usually so tense and so busy and only exercise, fucking and drinking relax me, but now I've discovered Grace and I can't get enough of her. Usually by now, I'd be bored with a woman, but not Grace. It's like the more I have of her, the more I want, and fuck me, it's terrifying. Moments like this, when we're not fucking but sitting quietly as we read the news on our phones, are sweet and enjoyable and I feel comfortable with her in a way I've never felt before.

While she reads, I steal glances at her, sweep my eyes over her heart-shaped face, her hair in its messy bun, her small, straight nose, her ample curves beneath one of my T-shirts, her naked shapely legs. Only once in my life has a woman got to me like this and it ended badly. I gave my heart then, and I swore I'd never do it again, but Grace is getting to me, making cracks in my veneer that allow her to reach inside and stroke my heart. I don't want it to happen and yet I do. I don't want to care about her and yet it's like I'm helpless to stop it from happening. I should create some distance between us, be cold towards her so she gets the message that we're done now, but that thought hurts my chest the way a kick from a horse would.

I know that this has to end and soon, before we both get in too deep. I can't allow myself to love her. I will end it.

But not today…

## Chapter 25

## *Grace*

The next day, I go about my life as normal but I can't help feeling different. This thing that's happening with Jack is so confusing. He's so tender and sweet; he made me breakfast yesterday following our incredible sex and then we sat together while we ate like a normal couple would do. We read the news, drank coffee, then went to get dressed for work. But of course that didn't go completely to plan, and we had sex again, me bent over the bed, with my skirt up around my waist and Jack naked from the waist down but wearing his shirt and tie. He's like a delicious addiction. My thoughts keep returning to what we said when we started this, though; we can't expect anything from each other because we both have baggage. I need to walk away soon, I know, before I get too involved, but I can't do it yet. I don't want to do it yet. For one thing, I'm having the best sex of my life and is it fair to stop cold turkey? Wouldn't that be me being mean to myself? Don't I deserve to keep enjoying him for a while longer?

I slept at home last night because Jack said he had a late meeting, but he did send me a text to say goodnight and then one to say good morning. Despite what we both said, we're acting like this is more than sex.

I descend the stairs of the flat and go through the private access door into the short hallway that leads to the café. I have some things to do this morning for Ava and Edward, and I'm keen to get started. But first, coffee...

By the time my stomach rumbles around noon, I've done what I needed to do that morning and can think about having some lunch. I close my laptop and go to the counter.

'You hungry yet?' Maisie asks.

'I am a bit.'

'Hold on.' She bends over behind the counter and reappears holding a picnic basket.

'What's that for?' I laugh.

'It's a beautiful day for a picnic. We thought you could call Jack and head to the park for lunch.'

'What? I can't expect him to meet me for lunch. He's working.'

'Grace, darling, everyone has to eat. Call him,' Riya says in her no-nonsense way. 'I packed some coffee and walnut cake, some macaroons and some fresh fruit and savouries. Have lunch with him on this gorgeous day.'

My aunt and Riya stare at me from behind the counter and I realise I can't turn my nose up at this lovely gesture. Besides which, it is a gorgeous day and it would be nice to have a picnic.

'OK then, I'll call him and see if he's free.'

To my surprise, Jack sounds keen and we agree to meet at Kyoto Garden in Holland Park in an hour.

'Here, have this too.' Maisie hands me a chilled bottle of rosé wine and two picnic mugs. 'It'll go nicely with the strawberries.'

'Are you two trying to marry me off or something?' Laughing, I shake my head because, of course, I know there's no way this is going to end in marriage. It will end with a wedding, but that wedding will be Ava and Edward's.

'We just want you to be happy.' Maisie smiles. 'And he seems to be making you happy.'

'He does,' Riya adds. 'You've been smiling a lot more lately. You like him, don't you?'

Glancing around the café to check no one's listening, I nod. 'I do, but it can't go anywhere.'

'Why not?' Maisie frowns.

'We agreed.'

'You agreed what?'

'That it would be temporary. It's better this way because we both know that we have no expectations other than enjoying our time together.'

Maisie and Riya exchange a look that makes me bristle. They've always done this when they think I'm being unreasonable.

'You can think what you like, but I'm taking care of my heart. If I don't fall for him, then I won't get hurt.'

The way they both stare at me convinces me they don't believe me at all, but it doesn't matter. What do they know? Then again, what do I know?

'Anyway, I'd better get going soon.' I make a point of looking at my smartwatch. 'I'm just going to change into something more picnic friendly.'

And to redo my hair and makeup and put on some decent lingerie, you know, just in case…

As I grab the picnic basket and carry it to the door marked *Private*, I hear them laughing softly and, in spite of myself, I smile too.

WHEN I GET to the park, I make my way to the Kyoto Garden. It's a beautiful spring day and the trees around the pond are reflected on the water's surface, making it look like there's a whole other world within the depths. It's such a lovely spot with stone lanterns, winding cobbled pathways, Japanese maple trees and cherry blossoms. Peacocks roam freely, the males flashing their tail feathers in glorious displays designed to attract the plainer females. It makes me think of Jack and how he's superior to me in the looks department. And yet he's never made me feel inferior. In fact, he makes me feel like I'm gorgeous and that's a first for me with a man. What if no one ever makes me feel that way again?

The picnic basket isn't light, so I find a bench and sit down, placing it on the bench next to me. It's so soothing here with the sound of the tiered waterfall, the birds singing, and a gentle breeze caressing my skin that I could close my eyes and take a nap.

'Hey, beautiful!'

I turn to see Jack approaching and smile as I admire how gorgeous he is. Whenever I see him, I find it hard to believe that he likes me and that I've slept with him. I mean, he *actually* likes me and wants to spend time with me.

'Hello.'

He comes around the bench and leans close, presses a kiss to my lips and it's a good thing I'm sitting down because my knees go weak. He smells incredible, and it's all I can do to stop myself from climbing onto his lap and wrapping myself around him. The way my body reacts to him stuns me every time because it's so visceral, so raw and primitive and unlike anything I've ever felt before. I could fall head over heels in love with this man if I didn't know better.

'How're you today?' he asks, his eyes crinkling at the corners. I see a flash of the man he'll be in twenty years and I know he'll look just as good in the way men this handsome do. What will he be like then, though? Married with kids? Still working as hard as he does now? I hope that whatever he is, he'll be happy.

'What're you thinking?' He frowns at me, a smile playing on his lips.

'What? Why?'

'You looked so serious then, like you had the worries of the world on your shoulders.'

'Oh, I don't know...'

'Tell me.' He reaches out and brushes a thumb over my cheek, and my heart thrums violently.

'I was wondering what you'll be like in twenty years.'

'And?' He cocks an eyebrow in a dangerously sexy manner.

'I hope that whatever you are, you'll be happy.'

He holds my gaze and his eyes bore deep into me. It's like he's scanning my brain, reaching into my soul to know me better and my breath catches in my throat. There's such intensity in his gaze that it causes me to tremble inwardly.

'You're the sweetest woman, Grace. I hope you'll be happy too and that whoever you're with treats you the way you deserve to be treated.'

Now I know that this thing between us is temporary, that there's no future in it, but his comment stings because he's reminding me that this isn't going anywhere, that he won't ever be the man in my life. I bite the inside of my cheek as tears burn at my eyes ridiculously, and look away to the waterfall, calming myself by focusing on the beauty of the scenery and taking myself away from this moment by looking outward rather than inward. But it's not lost on me that he doesn't think this will go anywhere, and it makes me wonder if it's because he doesn't think I'm good enough to imagine a future with. Just like my ex didn't.

'I think I'd better leave.' I go to stand up, but he catches my wrist and pulls me back.

'What's wrong?'

I can't look at him. 'Nothing.'

'Yes, there is. Grace, you invited me to a picnic and now you're going to leave before we've even eaten. What did I say?'

'Do you ... do you think I'm not good enough for you?'

'What?' He picks up the basket and moves it to the other side of him, then he slides towards me on the bench and takes my hand. 'Grace, why would you think that?'

'You speak of a future where we're not involved and I get that. I understand it because it's what we agreed. B-but then you say you hope I'll be with someone who makes me happy, and it makes me want to know ... Why?'

'Why what?'

'Why does it have to be someone else?'

'Grace, I work in a world where deals are brokered, contracts are signed and there's generally very little room for movement. Everything is black and white or it doesn't work. When we agree on something, we shake hands and sign on the dotted line and if anyone deviates from the contract, then the deal doesn't go down. If an employee doesn't meet their job description, then they're offered support. If they continue to fail to do their job properly then it often leads to capability procedures and even job loss.' He pushes his free hand through his thick hair and his scent washes over me, weakens me further. 'We agreed that this would be physical and to me that seemed risk free. I have baggage and I'm not always a good person. I can't be what you need me to be and I hate to disappoint anyone.'

'How do you know what I need?'

He shakes his head. 'I don't, not really, but you're a kind person and you deserve the best in life and love. I can give you that physically but emotionally ... I don't think I could measure up. Although our time together has been limited, I know that you're incredible. You're funny, smart, and kind, you're amazing in bed and you're the hottest women I've ever had the pleasure of seeing naked. If anyone's not good enough, it's me. I don't deserve you because I can't be the type of man who can make you happy.'

It's my turn to shake my head now because I don't agree with what he's saying and yet, it rings true. When you've been through difficult times, it's hard to see yourself as a whole person who has enough to give to another and to a relationship. I like Jack and I love spending time with him, but after what I've been through, am I really capable of giving myself to him? It's a risk that could go very wrong. It could go well, but my experience of relationships is that they go badly and what if this did too? I'd be even more damaged than before. This no-strings sex means that we get to enjoy each other without the risk and so, really, the sensible option is to enjoy it and to forget about the future. After all, worrying will only ruin what we have right here and now.

'OK then. But I don't think we can go on indefinitely like this.'

'So what are you suggesting?' He raises my hand to his mouth and kisses my fingers one by one. His lips are soft and the tiny kisses make the hairs on my arms rise. He turns my hand over and kisses my wrist, inhales as if he can get high from my scent. When he kisses up my arm to the inside of my elbow, I moan softly. An elderly couple walk past and the woman's eyes widen when she looks at Jack kissing me, but then she smiles and takes her companion's hand as if inspired by what she saw.

'I'm suggesting that we have a deadline.'

'A deadline?'

'Yes. So we know when this is over. That way there's no room for error and we both fulfil the terms of our contract without getting hurt or confused. The lines of our agreement won't be blurred if this thing between us has an end date.' I sound so practical and sensible, but the thought of waking up one day and saying goodbye to Jack leaves a sour taste on my tongue.

'When are you thinking?'

'How about the wedding day?'

He laughs. 'Our wedding day?'

'What?' I splutter. 'No, of course not. I meant Ava and Edward's.'

'Of course.' He nods vigorously. 'Of course that's what you meant. But ... that doesn't leave us long. Just over a week, in fact.'

'It's a sensible amount of time so we don't get too involved.'

'Right. OK.' He stares across the park and I notice a tiny muscle in his jaw twitching. 'If that's what you want.'

'It's what we both want, isn't it?'

He inclines his head and then he presses a kiss to my palm as if to seal the deal.

'Now, shall we eat? Riya packed us the most amazing picnic.'

'Let's go over there and sit on the grass.' He gestures across the park to a spot under two adjacent blossom trees.

When we're sitting on the soft grass, he removes his jacket and places it behind us. 'You can lean on my jacket,' he says.

'It will get grass stains on it.' I shake my head.

'It's fine. It's an older one, anyway. Shall I get everything out of the basket?'

I nod, then turn and peer at the jacket and touch the material. It feels expensive. It doesn't look old at all, but I don't want to ruin this moment, so I lean on the jacket and wait while he unpacks our lunch.

First, he pulls out a checked tablecloth that I didn't see Riya pack. He lays it on the grass, then puts tubs of things on top. There are fat, shiny green olives with small slices of lemon; sundried tomatoes in olive oil; crusty bread; pale, soft butter; a block of gouda with a golden rind; a round coffee and walnut cake; pink and yellow macaroons and fat, red strawberries. There's also the wine that he opens and pours into the two mugs.

'Cheers.' He taps his mug against mine and I take a sip. 'It tastes like summer and also like something else I could mention.' He winks at me and I frown in question.

'Your sweet, pink pussy.' He walks the fingers of his right hand up my thigh and rests the hand at the top, and my core tingles.

'You're saying I taste like rosé?'

'Like strawberries, melon, raspberries ... like champagne and summer... You're delicious, Grace. You have no idea how delicious. I could eat you all day long.'

Heat floods my face, and I sip my wine again. He could eat me all day long. No man has ever said that to me before. Jack has a way of making me feel special, like I matter and like I'm beautiful. I like how I feel when I'm with him. What a shame this has to end.

We work our way through the picnic while the breeze shakes the blossom trees and soft, pink petals drift down around us. Jack tells me about the type of things he does at work and then asks me about weddings I've helped plan. The food is delicious; the wine makes me feel relaxed and floaty, and the company is wonderful.

After we've finished eating, Jack packs what's left of the food in the basket and pours the rest of the wine in our mugs. We lie side by side on his jacket and gaze up at the canopy created by the branches and petals of the blossom trees. Patches of blue sky appear every time the breeze caresses the blossom and a few puffy, white clouds float overhead. It is a perfect day, and this is a perfect moment in time, and if I've never understood the importance of living in the moment before, I understand perfectly now.

Jack moves closer to me and rests his head on my chest, and I run my fingers through his hair. His right arm is draped over my waist, his left one tucked behind, and with each breath I take, his head rises and falls. It takes a few minutes for me to realise that he's fallen asleep and so I hold him close, this lovely, lovely man. We might not have the future, or even the rest of the day, as we both need to get back to work, but we have here and now that's enough for me.

# Chapter 26

## *Jack*

Sitting in a meeting a few hours after the picnic with Grace, my mind is anywhere other than on the presentation a junior colleague is making about financial forecasts for the next quarter. I have tried to focus, but the wine and the sunny extended lunchtime spent in the beautiful gardens have relaxed me. Drinking at lunchtime isn't something I usually indulge in — unless it's a special business lunch — because I'd want to nap the afternoon away, but the rosé was delicious. As delicious as Grace ... I loved seeing her blush when I said it tasted like her. She really does taste delicious. I remember reading once that someone's smell and taste only work for you if the pheromones are right, and with Grace they must be, because I could eat her all day long.

*Oops!*

There's movement south of the border at the thought of burying my face in her delicious pussy and tasting her sweetness again. I can't think about that now, so I'd better focus on Giovanni's graphs. I don't need a stonking erection in a business meeting, do I? If I stand up right now, Giovanni will think it's him I've got the hots for.

*Come on, Jack, focus ... Numbers. Graphs. Next quarter.*

*Grace...*

*Oh Grace...*

And she said she wondered if I thought she wasn't good enough for me. Absolute insanity! I'd love to know what stupid fuckwad made her believe she wasn't anything other than incredible. I could happily rip his head from his shoulders and use it as a bowling ball.

'Jack?' Giovanni is staring at me and I shift in my seat. 'Did you have something to add or a question?' He raises his perfectly shaped dark brows at me in that way he has, and I clear my throat.

'Nope. All looks about right to me.'

'Oh...' Giovanni's hands flutter briefly, then settle on his hips. He's very keen to impress and was clearly hoping I was going to offer some praise on his report.

'Excellent report though, G,' I say. 'Plenty of information we can use there. Right, Edward?'

My friend turns in his chair and smiles at me, a quizzical frown marring his brow. Probably because I'm waffling. Nothing I just said has any real weight. 'Absolutely agree, Jack. Well done, Giovanni.'

We turn back to face Giovanni, and he basks in the glow of our praise. Some managers underestimate the weight of praise, but it goes a long way and inspires employee loyalty that lasts. Who doesn't like to be told they're doing a good job? No one I've ever met, that's for sure.

'Thank you.' Giovanni bobs his head, then turns back to the giant touchscreen in the boardroom on our floor.

While he finishes his presentation, my phone buzzes in my pocket and I pull it out under the table and sneak a peek, hoping it's Grace. Instead, I see a message from Edward:

**WTF was that? Your head is somewhere else, buddy, and I'm guessing it's with a lady.**

I bite back a smile and reply:

**Never! I'm a consummate professional.**

Edward responds with a laughing emoji and I send one in return.

Twenty minutes later, Giovanni has finished his presentation and everyone's filing out of the boardroom.

'Could I have a word, Jack?' Edward says, closing the door so we're alone. 'Everything all right?'

'Fine.' I nod and lean against the table, slip my hands into my trouser pockets.

'You sure?' He walks over to me and reaches around my jacket and pulls his hand back, peering at something he's holding. 'You had grass on your jacket.'

I snigger. 'I had a picnic lunch.'

'That's what you're calling it these days, is it?'

'Seriously. I went for lunch with Grace in the Kyoto Garden. It was really nice. Her aunt made a picnic, and we sat on the grass and ate and talked.'

Edward licks his lips and takes a slow breath. 'You like her, don't you?'

I look down at the floor, then back up at my friend. 'I do.'

'So what're you going to do about it?'

'Nothing.'

'What? But why not? I haven't seen you like this about anyone since ... well, you know.'

'We've agreed to keep it to strictly pleasure and enjoying each other and then we'll go our separate ways.'

'But why?' He's frowning now and shaking his head. 'If you've met someone you really like, why would you end it?'

Rubbing a hand over my beard, I sigh. 'We both have baggage. Me especially. And neither of us wants to bring that into something that would end up with us getting hurt. Most likely her. At least this way we can have some fun and not get emotionally involved.'

'So you're not involved or at all invested? I know you, Jack, and I can see that this woman is different. She's not your usual *type*.' He uses air quotes around *type*. 'Grace is a nice person. She's hardworking and sweet and kind and Ava really likes her. I would hate to see her, or you, get hurt. Therefore, I don't understand why you'd make this temporary.'

'Like you with your marriage contract?' I fire back and Edward winces.

'OK. That wasn't my best plan but I needed to find a way around the inheritance clause in my grandfather's will. You know this.'

'I do and I'm sorry. That was uncalled for. You're just looking out for me.'

'I am.' He pats my arm. 'I really am. You were hurt before, and I understand that more than most. God knows I was hurt too, but look at me now.'

'All loved up with your perfect woman,' I reply.

'Exactly. If I'd shut Ava out, I'd be broken, and who would that help? Not me. Not Ava. Not Joe. I have everything now and I'm so glad I took a chance. You should too.'

He's being kind and a loyal friend, I know this, but my circumstances are different.

'We've agreed to end it after your wedding.'

'So you're going to distract our wedding planner up to that point and then dump her?'

'Not dump her ... We just won't carry on.'

'Jack, man, I saw you at the club. I saw how you reacted when that scumbag hit on her. Do you really think you'll be able to walk away and not care if she sees someone else? If someone else hurts her? This woman means something to you and you'd be mad to let her go.'

I shrug. 'Maybe. But we've agreed.'

'Is it what she wants?'

'She said it is.'

'I think you're mad, but it's your life. Just think about it a bit more though, please? If you let her go, I have a feeling you'll live to regret it.'

He pats my arm again, then walks to the door and opens it. 'In other news ... I was wondering how your best man's speech is coming along?'

*Shit! I'd completely forgotten about that.*

'Brilliantly!' I smile. 'You're going to love it.'

'Can't wait.' He grins at me, then leaves the boardroom and I watch as he walks along the corridor to his office and disappears inside.

I've been so distracted by everything that I'd forgotten about the speech. Lucas will need to write one too, but knowing him, his will be far more risqué than anything I'd dare to compose. I guess I'd better get my head around what I want to say, but where do I start? I wonder if Grace can help?

# Chapter 27

## *Grace*

'Cut it out.' I giggle and push Jack's hand away reluctantly. We're at a London restaurant in a corner booth. There's low lighting, candles on the tables, wine in our glasses and jazz plays from invisible speakers. He phoned this morning to invite me to meet him for dinner because he had something to ask me. Turns out it was for help with his best man's speech. And right now I'm trying to focus as I help him to write it. I have a notepad on the table in front of me, a pen in my hand and he's meant to be brainstorming his thoughts and feelings — about Edward, Ava and their relationship and about what Jack thinks love is. The latter I'm particularly keen to hear about because it's quite significant in terms of the baggage he keeps mentioning.

'Grace, I can't concentrate when I'm near you,' he says, running his hand back up my leg and underneath the hem of my skirt. When his fingertips caress the top of my stocking, a thrill shoots through me. I glance around the restau-

*Healing the Billionaire's Heart*

rant, but no one's taking any notice of us. 'I want you all the time.'

'You said you wanted some help with your speech,' I say, wriggling as his hand moves from my thigh to my panties.

'You're wet,' he growls as he strokes me, pushing the satin of my lingerie against my folds. It makes me gasp because I am aroused. How could I not be when this prince of a man is so close, when he's touching me and telling me he wants me? When he slips his finger under the satin and makes contact with my clit, I shiver in delight. 'Incredibly wet.'

'Jack...' I can't hold back much longer.

'Don't you come now, you naughty Goldie,' he says, increasing the speed of his touch.

'Stop then!' My voice wavers because I don't want him to stop and yet he should. We're in a public place for crying out loud.

'Really?'

'Yes. No. Uggghhhh.' I moan as I come against his fingertip and he keeps stroking me gently until the last of my orgasm flutters through me.

'Again?' he asks.

'What?' I squeak. 'Now?'

He slides a finger inside me and another then he uses the pad of his thumb to caress my swollen clit.

'I can't.' I meet his eyes, but his pupils are dilated, and it's like he's not there. He's become lust. Become need. Become want.

'Yes, you can.' His fingers go deeper and his thumb rubs over me. I push my shoes into the carpet beneath the table as he drives me closer to pleasure. 'That's it. Ride me like that.'

And I do. I am his captive, trapped in the corner of the seat, trapped between him and the table. If I wanted to move, I couldn't and his fingers feel so good, his thumb is massaging me just right and...

'Jack!' I shatter again and again as he holds me with his one hand beneath my skirt.

When he gently pulls out of me, I slump onto the seat. Realising that I'm still holding the pen, I laugh, especially when I see the jagged line I've drawn up the page. 'You are so bad.'

He holds his hand in front of his face, then slowly licks his fingers. 'Just like fucking rosé wine,' he says. 'Now, help me get this speech done.'

We write and eat and sip the velvety red wine from large blue glass goblets. Jack entertains me with funny stories about his friendship with Edward and Lucas, and I gain a better insight into what they mean to one another and the business they've built together. It might have been Edward's family business, but since they started working for Cavendish Construction, Edward, Jack and Lucas have run it like a family. They are friends but as good as brothers.

Jack also tells me about Ava and Edward and how broken Edward was before Ava came along. They'd told me their own version of events, but it's always interesting to hear another version, that of an observer who cares for them both. Jack thinks Ava has saved Edward from the desolation

*Healing the Billionaire's Heart*

he felt after losing his first wife, and I can understand that. Edward would have been OK, but now he has Ava, he's more than OK. He has joy in his life again and that's what finding your person can do for you. It can give you more than you ever imagined in your life. It's a beautiful story and I'm so happy to be involved in helping to create their happy ever after.

'Right, I think we have quite a lot to work with,' I say as I put the pen down.

'Cheers to that.' Jack picks up his glass and clinks it against mine. 'Thank you so much, Grace. You helped me a lot with that. I'll draft it and then see what you think if that's OK?'

'Of course. I'm happy to help.' And I am, but the thought that each day takes us closer to the wedding is bittersweet because it will mean the union of two of the loveliest people I've ever met, but also the end of me and Jack. The end of us and whatever it is that we have between us.

Jack sets his glass down, then stands up. 'Come with me a moment?' He steps out of the booth and holds out his hand.

Taking it, I stand too and he leads me to the rear of the restaurant and through a door. We walk along a short corridor and then he pushes a door to the left and turns on a light. We're in some sort of storage room, I realise, as he closes the door behind us. There are shelves of napkins and tablecloths, boxes of candles and glasses. It smells like vanilla and lemon furniture polish.

'What are we doing in here?' I ask.

'I need you.' He pushes me backwards until I can feel the cold metal of a shelf against my back through my blouse. He places his hands on my breasts and cups them. 'Your tits are the best I've ever seen.' Lowering his head, he bites at my hard nipples through the satin blouse and the lace of my bra beneath and I shudder.

'We can't do this here,' I say, but I want to.

'We can do whatever we want.' He unbuttons my blouse and parts it, then lowers his head and sucks at my nipples through my bra. I know I should probably tell him we need to return to our table, but I'm breathless with desire and I want to find out what he's going to do next. He intrigues me because I've never been with a man like him before. So when he grabs my skirt and pulls it up, I don't fight. 'I can smell your arousal,' he says, reaching down. He pushes my panties aside and rubs the back of his fingers over me. 'Still fucking soaking.'

I can't take it anymore and I grab at his zipper, release his erection from his trousers and trunks, and rub the tip over my clit while he tears the foil on a condom. He hands it to me and I roll it down his shaft, and then he's inside me in one thrust.

It's fast and hard and he comes quickly, groaning into my shoulder, his hands gripping my bottom so tight he's going to leave bruises. I don't even mind because they'll be bruises from the pleasure we give each other.

'Now you,' he says as he pulls out of me.

'It's OK.' Shaking my head, I touch his face. 'I came already, remember?'

'I never want to leave my woman unsatisfied.'

*Healing the Billionaire's Heart*

He tidies his trousers, then drops to his knees and wraps my legs around his shoulders. I gasp when he buries his face between my thighs, sucking on my clit until I erupt over his face, bucking against him while I grip his hair.

It's only afterwards, while we rearrange our clothing, that it dawns on me what he said…

'I never want to leave *my woman* unsatisfied.'

## Chapter 28

### *Jack*

'Darling, it's so good to see you.' My mother stands up at the table and embraces me, cloaking me in a cloud of Chanel No.5.

'Hi, Mum,' I reply, kissing both her cheeks. 'You look good.'

She laughs and sits down while I hug my father and exchange awkward pats on the back.

When we're done, I pull out my chair and sit at the round table. It's very different from the corner booth Grace and I shared yesterday and thinking of her sends a pang though me I suspect might be because she's not here. But then why would she be here? She's not my girlfriend or partner or anything other than someone I fuck. Right?

'You do look good, Mum. I don't know why you always dismiss me when I tell you that.'

And she does. I mean, the woman has been through hell and come back with her signature fighting spirit. Nothing seems to get her down, and she keeps on going, no matter what.

'I tell her every day how gorgeous she is,' my dad says, tenderly brushing a hand over Mum's cheek. 'But she tells me to stop talking nonsense, too.' He holds up his hands and shrugs. 'I will not stop telling her, though.'

A waiter appears at the table so we order a bottle of wine and then peruse the menus.

'Lovely restaurant, darling,' Mums say over the top of her menu. 'Why have we never been here before?'

'Because it's new,' Dad says. 'Remember?'

Mum nods. 'Of course. Silly me.' She laughs and Dad smiles fondly at her.

They've always been this way: close, caring, adoring and they've been married for over forty years, which to me seems crazy. How can you be with someone for that long and not get bored or irritated by them? It's one of the things about relationships that scares me, the thought of committing to someone then getting fed up of them. But I guess if it's the right person, then that won't happen. My parents are the perfect example of this.

After we've ordered, I raise my wine glass. 'Here's to family and wishing you a very happy birthday, Dad.'

We clink glasses and then drink. It's a good wine, red and robust and will go perfectly with the steak I've ordered.

'Thanks, son.' Dad grins at me. 'I can't believe I'm 65.'

'Not until tomorrow, Daniel,' Mum reminds him.

'Yes, but almost,' he says.

'How are things in the world of law?' I ask, setting my glass on the table.

'Oh, you know…' Dad combs his thick, white moustache with his fingers. 'Pretty much the same.'

'He still speaks to his former colleagues almost every day.' Mum rolls her eyes. 'He's meant to be retired, but it's like an addiction for him.

I do know. Dad retired from his job as a criminal lawyer two years ago, but you wouldn't know it. He can't seem to leave his career behind, and I can't blame him. He loved his job, and the firm he worked for was a huge part of his life for so long. Mum wanted him to retire because the long hours were hard on him and she thought he should have some quality of life. However, it appears that Dad enjoyed his job far more than we realised, and so he keeps in touch with his former colleagues and helps when he can with advice. I wonder if he'll ever walk away fully and doubt that he will. It's a big part of who he is and it's the same with me, I think. I love my job and am usually immersed in it, but recently, well, let's be honest, since I met Grace, I've definitely been distracted. She's just so different from any woman I've been with. I actually like her and that's what stuns me most.

'What about you, Jack?' Dad asks. 'Anything to report about work?'

I update them on recent projects and future proposals, and they show their usual keen interest that they've always shown in me and my brothers. They are and always have been wonderful parents.

*Healing the Billionaire's Heart*

'And how are Edward and Lucas?' Mum asks.

'Both are well. Edward is looking forward to getting married and Lucas is ... well, enjoying himself as per usual.'

Mum sips her wine, but I can see that her brain is whirring. 'Isn't it lovely that Edward's getting married? I know he's been through some tough times, but now he's found himself a new bride and he's going to have a mother for his little boy.'

'Ava is wonderful with Joe.' I nod. 'I'm sure they will all be very happy together.'

'If only ...' Mum sighs theatrically and gazes across the restaurant. Dad catches my eye and winks. 'If only you could find someone.'

'Mum ...' I suppress my frustration as best I can. 'I did have someone, and it didn't work out and I just don't feel that it's what I want now.' Am I telling the truth, though? Grace has definitely reached part of me — ahem, in more ways than one — that no one else has reached, at least not for some time. I know I care about her and that I'll miss her when we go our separate ways, but that doesn't mean that we should consider an alternative. We both have baggage that could have serious implications for any relationship we might have and so it's just not worth thinking about anything long-term.

'I'd love for you to get married and have children.' Mum's eyes glisten and my heart aches for her. I know how much she wants to see me settled and I wish it was something I could give her. But this isn't just about Mum's happiness, it's about Grace's and mine too and it's all so ... complicated. I know how upset Mum was when things didn't work out with Lara and I couldn't bear for that to happen again. 'I'd love to be a grandmother and to spend time with some little ones that look just like you, my handsome boy.' She leans her chin on her hands and stares down at her plate.

I love my mum so much, but I know from a lifetime of experience that she's good at pulling at the heartstrings. She knows how to get to me and my brothers as she's perfected the craft with my dad. Never in a bad way, but when she wants something for us — and it's *always* about our happiness — she knows how to work the emotion.

'I'm sorry, Mum. Maybe one day.'

She meets my eyes across the table and inclines her head. 'I really hope so because I only want the best for you.'

'I know.'

The rest of dinner passes with Mum and Dad telling me about a cruise they have planned in the autumn and about the walking they've done recently. They both love hiking in the Lake District and around the UK. It keeps them fit and Mum has even done a few sponsored walks to raise money for cancer charities. Her resilience and determination will never cease to amaze and inspire me. She's also incredibly kind and compassionate and there's something about Grace that's very similar. They're both strong women who are considerate of others and who shine because of their good hearts. I never thought I'd meet a woman who shone like my mother, but I have and despite this, I'm convinced I have to let her go. It'll be for her own good at the end of the day because I don't have the freedom to give myself these days, and Grace really deserves far better than that. In fact, she deserves to have a man who'd give her the entire world.

# Chapter 29

## *Grace*

In the hotel lobby, I check my list again. A week has passed since Jack and I had our picnic and I can't believe how quickly the days have gone. I think I've done everything I needed to for today and tomorrow, but the fear that I might have missed something will always be present, keeping me on my toes.

Hearing voices, I look up the winding staircase and smile. *There she is...*

As Ava descends the staircase with her mum, I can't take my eyes off her. She's a beautiful young woman and in her wedding rehearsal outfit of floaty peach dress and matching sandals with a peach rose in her hair, she's breath-taking. Knowing what her wedding dress is like, I can't wait to see her tomorrow too.

When she reaches the bottom of the stairs, she opens her arms and hugs me.

'I can't believe it's my wedding eve.' Her eyes glow with excitement.

'It has come around quickly,' I reply. 'How are you feeling?'

'Good.' She nods, but her smile falters and I wonder what it is. Nerves probably, I've seen enough brides in my time to know that nerves can kick in even when getting married is exactly what a woman wants. Her eyes slide left towards Nancy and I realise she doesn't want to say anything in front of her. 'Where's Daniel?' she asks her mum.

Nancy looks around with a frown as if she might have misplaced him in the hotel somewhere. 'I thought he was with Jeff.' Then she nods. 'He is with Jeff. They were going for a walk around the grounds so Daniel could burn off some steam before dinner.'

'Excellent.' Ava chews at her bottom lip.

'I might just go and powder my nose, actually,' Nancy says, opening her clutch bag and peering inside it.

'I'll meet you on the terrace,' Ava says.

When Nancy is gone, I take Ava's arm. 'Is everything really OK?'

She sighs and blinks her amber eyes at me. 'Kind of.'

'What is it?' I lean closer.

'I'm just a bit tired, I think.' She doesn't meet my gaze when she says this and I gather there's more to it but don't want to press her. If she wants to talk at some point, she will.

'Well, I'm here for you, anything you need.' I smile at her and the briefest of smiles crosses her lips.

'Thanks. You've been amazing, Grace. Really amazing. I'm so glad we contacted you because I'd never have sorted all this alone. Not only have you organised the wedding, you've ensure that the lead up to it ran smoothly and that we have everything we need.'

'It's my job.' I wrap my arm around her shoulders and hug her. 'And a pleasure. I want you to have the wedding you always dreamt of having. When you walk down that aisle tomorrow, I want you to relax and enjoy your big day.'

She lets out a small gasp and then covers her face. 'Sorry ... I h-have to ... excuse me.'

I'm about to follow her when Jack and Lucas enter the hotel.

'Hey there, gorgeous.' Jack comes to my side and strokes my bare arm gently and my body responds immediately.

'Hey there.' I meet his gorgeous eyes and smile.

'Don't mind me,' Lucas says, smirking.

'Hi Lucas,' I kiss his cheeks.

'How's it going?' he asks me, his piercing blue eyes scanning my face. I feel heat filling my cheeks and curse myself inwardly. It's not that I fancy Lucas because I don't. As attractive as I know he is, it's because he's one of those men who really looks at women as if they can see deep down inside them, and it's unnerving.

'Good, thanks. The other guests have gone through to the terrace,' I say, hoping he'll catch my meaning. I don't want to be rude, but I'd like a moment with Jack before I go and find Ava.

'Cool.' Lucas says, cocking an eyebrow. His salt and pepper hair is slicked back from his tanned forehead and his square jaw is dusted with matching stubble. He's tall and broad shouldered like Jack and Edward and it's like someone designed them to be a trio of friends. They could be models or celebrities, grace the covers of magazines with their handsome faces and expensive clothes. 'Catch you soon.' He bobs his head at Jack, then leaves us alone.

'Hey,' Jack says now as he steps closer. When he leans forwards and kisses my cheeks, my knees weaken.

'Hey,' I reply, wanting to wrap my arms around his waist but holding back because I'm working and we're not officially together, so it wouldn't be good for people to see me hugging him. I say *not officially* together, and the thought turns me cold all over because we're not and never will be. Who knows, maybe one day I could plan Jack's wedding to a woman he feels he can put his baggage aside for.

'Nice hotel,' he says, looking around at the antique furniture that fills the great hallway, the wide staircase, and the chandeliers that sparkle above.

'I've been to a few weddings here. It's a perfect setting for a wedding or rehearsal dinner.'

Nodding, he takes me by surprise as he slides his arm around my waist and pulls me close. The way he holds me against him is proprietorial and I like it, even though I know this can't happen here and now.

'Jack!' I place a hand on his shirt front, feel the rock-hard abs beneath it and the power in the arm that's pinning me against him.

'Weddings you planned?' he asks.

'Yes.' I press my lips together, straining against his arm, but he wraps the other one around me and squeezes me tight. 'Jack ... people will see.'

'So?'

'This is my job. I need to be professional.'

He scans my face, then releases me and I step back. 'Of course. I'm sorry. It's just that every time I see you, I want to hold you.'

Biting back a retort about us not having much time left, I swallow hard. This is not the time for anger or tears. I know the score and have done since we first spent time together.

'I need to look for Ava.' I check my iPad as if she might have messaged me. Well, she might, but really, it's just for something to do.

'Is everything all right?' His thick brows meet above his straight nose.

'Fine,' I reply quickly. 'Just a few last-minute things to check.'

'I'll leave you to it, then.' His eyes are filled with questions, and I have to look away. He's like a drug and I need to wean myself off him gradually. Otherwise, after the wedding, I'm going to have to go cold turkey and it will be too much. Far better to accept now that we're not going anywhere with this, that it's just been a fling and neither of us is in the market for more. I'm torn between anger at him for not putting up a fight for me and shaking my head at myself because I told him I wanted nothing serious. I'm a walking contradiction. Being sensible is what's needed but I love who I am when I'm with him, and I love the way he makes me feel. Walking away from this — from us — will be the hardest thing I've ever had to do.

'Great.' The smile I force to my lips is as false as the nonchalance in my tone. But what else can I do? How else can I behave when Jack is not and never will be mine?

Forcing myself to stare at my iPad as he walks away, I swallow the urge to call him back. It's high time for me to get a grip and, most importantly, to focus on doing my job! I will not allow another man to ruin my business or to break my heart.

When I'm sure he's gone, I lower my iPad and slip it into my bag then head after Ava. There's something wrong with her and I need to find out what.

# Chapter 30

## *Grace*

I hurry through the hallway and pass under an archway to the drawing room. There are windows to my right and an enormous fireplace to my left. Straight ahead are French doors framed by thick velvet curtains. Ava isn't in here, but I'm sure she came in this direction. I walk through the room and to the door in the rear wall.

The panelled door, made of dark wood, looks heavy. I take the handle, twist it and push and find myself in what must be some sort of antechamber. It's cool and dark and smells like incense and there's a faint hint of Ava's perfume.

Ahead of me is another door and to my left is empty shelving. Part of me longs to get out of the enclosed space, but I have to find Ava and can't go back to the guests without her. Of course, she might have already gone to them, but if she hasn't and I turn up without her, then it's going to arouse suspicion about where she is and why she isn't with me.

Reaching out, I touch the shelving. It gives beneath my palm and I find myself at the foot of a winding staircase.

Ava's perfume is stronger here, so I start to climb, my heels clicking on the stone steps. My breathing is audible because the air is musty and because I'm anxious about where I'm going. I'm not a fan of confined spaces and just about every horror movie I've ever seen flashes through my head. If I was watching a movie character do this, I'd be shouting at her to go back and not let curiosity kill the cat. But it's not a movie and I have a job to do and I need to find the bride.

Before long, I find myself on a small landing. This hotel used to be a family home and clearly has lots of secret passageways and dark corners. How Ava knew where to go is beyond me, but then perhaps she was too upset to care. I'm certain now that she was upset and that it's serious. She doesn't seem like the type of person to do something for drama's sake, so there must be a reason she's set off through these narrow spaces.

I decide to try the door to my right and when I push; it opens into a small room with a window overlooking the courtyard at the centre of the building. Below on the grass, a wood pigeon is bobbing its head as it shuffles along. A noise behind me makes me whirl around and then I see her slumped over her knees in a chair.

'Ava?' Approaching her as I would a wounded animal, hands outstretched, I crouch in front of her. 'What's wrong? Please tell me.'

When she raises her head, I see the state of her makeup and am filled with dismay.

'I-I ... I'm scared.'

'Oh, love.' I rub at her icy hands and take them in mine. 'That's perfectly natural. I've known so many brides feel that way when the wedding actually arrives. Tomorrow will be a big day for you and some nerves are natural. Marriage is a big commitment.' One that's too big for some people, I think, based on my own experience, but I don't say this because it's not what she needs to hear right now.

'N-no.' She sniffs and I pull a tissue from my pocket and hand it to her. 'I'm not scared of getting married s-so much, but of ... not being enough.'

'Sweetheart, you are more than enough.'

I lean forwards and hug her. Stroke her soft hair.

'You are everything to Edward and he loves you. I've never seen a man look at a woman that way before.'

'Really?' she asks.

'I promise you.' I lean back and smile at her.

'It all happened so quickly between us ... me being the nanny and then falling in love with Edward and some days, I have to pinch myself. But then I think ... what if he only fell for me because I was there and I'm not actually the right person for him?' The worry in her pretty eyes makes me want to wrap her up in cotton wool and look after her.

'Have you spoken to Edward about these concerns? I'm sure he'd put your mind at ease,' I say, brushing a lock of hair behind her ear.

'I've been so busy with the wedding preparation and so afraid that this might all blow up in my face that I haven't told him,' she admits. 'Plus, there's the clause in his grandfather's will that states Edward has to be married on his thirty-fifth birthday or he can't become permanent CEO of

Cavendish Construction or inherit majority shares in the business. So he needs to marry me even if he has doubts.'

'Ava,' I say, taking her hands in mine. 'These are natural worries in light of how you came to be together, but I've seen you and Edward, and he loves you. I have no doubt about it at all. The man is besotted with you and would be devastated if he knew you were having these worries.'

She holds my gaze, a million emotions flickering through her eyes, and then she sighs and seems to release something from her slim frame. 'It's hard to trust in love when you've never had it before.'

'I can imagine. It's hard to trust in love at the best of times, but trusting others is a choice we make.' My words sound so wise, but I know first-hand how difficult it is to trust someone and how hard I would find it if I was in Ava's shoes. 'It's a choice we make every day and one that won't always come easily, but I think it's worth making that choice for love.'

'You do?' Her eyes scan my face and I pray I won't reveal a hint of my doubts. I want her to be happy, and I truly believe that Edward loves her and genuinely wants to spend the rest of his life with her.

'I do.' I pull her to her feet and into a hug, then lean back and meet her gaze again. 'You are an amazing woman and you should have faith in yourself. You deserve to be loved, you know?'

'I struggle sometimes to believe that, and Edward is so amazing. He could have anyone.'

'The thing is though, Ava, he only wants you.'

Her smile lights up her face and warmth rushes through me. Thank goodness I said the right thing, and she's looking happier.

'How about we go down to the hallway and I find Edward for you? I think you should speak to him about this because he needs to know that you're feeling vulnerable.'

'I don't want to dampen his excitement.'

'I don't think that's possible. That man is ecstatic about marrying you tomorrow and I think knowing that you're feeling vulnerable will just allow him to reassure you.'

'You're right,' she says with a nod. 'Let's go and find him.'

We head back down to the main hall and while she pops to the ladies' to freshen her makeup; I find Edward. He's concerned, but I tell him it's nothing to worry about, just a few nerves because she loves him and he seems comforted by that. I know that nerves are natural the day before and day of your wedding, but if two people truly love each other, then they can find their way through those nerves to make a commitment that will hopefully endure. For Ava and Edward, it will all work out and I'm so sure of that I'd stake my favourite shoes on it.

Taking a deep breath, I stride in the direction of the terrace. I need to ensure that everything is running smoothly and to direct the guests to the dining room, where they will eat the rehearsal meal. I'm glad I opted out of food though, because the knot in my stomach is so tight I wouldn't be able to force so much as a spoonful of soup down.

## Chapter 31

### *Jack*

After leaving Grace, I marched out to the terrace and grabbed a flute of champagne off a passing server. I threw it down my throat, then went in search of another before pacing around the lawn like a madman. For fuck's sake, what is wrong with me? Grace gave me the cold shoulder and I'm stressed out about it. I know this is her job, and she has to remain professional and yet I still tried to kiss and cuddle her in a place where anyone could have seen her. Why would I do that? Why would I risk her reputation and her business just because I couldn't keep my hands to myself? She'll think I'm an absolute idiot now and I can't blame her. What kind of man does that to a woman he cares about?

When I've imbibed another glass of champagne, I look around and see a group of other guests gathering for photographs. A few of the young women are all dressed up and looking good, so I wander over to them and join their conversation. They're happy to include me, and soon things get flirtatious in the way they do when I'm around single women who find rich men attractive. It's an easy routine and I know it off by heart and soon, one of them is leaning in close and pressing her satin clad breasts against my arm. Her perfume is musky and something I'd normally like, but this evening all I can think is that she doesn't smell like Grace. She doesn't look like Grace either. Her breasts are small and high, not like Grace's large heavy tits that sway when we fuck. Just the thought of those tits makes me hard. The woman speaking to me tilts her head as if gazing towards the sun and I listen to her story about ... well, I have no idea what it's about because I'm bored. But hey ... she's cute enough to screw, and so when she moves to her toes and whispers in my ear that she'd like me to take her doggy style, I grin. I'm about to reply with a comment about smacking her tight ass for being such a bad girl when I look up and spot Grace on the terrace steps. She's staring right at me and my companion, and my heart sinks. I'd step backwards but there's a hedge right behind me and so I try to tell her with my eyes that there's nothing going on here, nothing to worry about, but her expression tells me all I need to know. Grace would not piss on me right now if I was on fire and I can't say I blame her. Perhaps this is for the best anyway, because we were due to end things tomorrow. Perhaps this is the plaster being ripped off quickly in order to cause us less pain.

*Wait ... pain?*

Not pain, because it's not like I love her or anything. I'm simply fond of her and like spending time with her. And fucking her, of course.

She turns on her heel and disappears into a crowd of people and I'm left on the lawn with this woman whose name I don't even recall and she's attached to my arm like a vice. Her nails are long and painted scarlet to match her lips and I suspect that if I don't shake her off soon, that same colour lipstick will be on my cock.

Why is it that the thought of that turns me cold? Usually, it would be something I'd look forward to, but not anymore, it seems.

Not. Anymore.

Something is very wrong with me ...

# Chapter 32

## *Grace*

The guests have taken their seats at the horseshoe table in the dining room, and I'm hovering at the periphery, waiting and watching to ensure that all goes well. Serving staff bustle past me, delivering starters to tables and others circulate with trays of wine and soft drinks. In the corner, a string quartet plays covers of love songs from over the years and the mood is one of romance and joy. Ava and Edward are all smiles and he can barely take his eyes off her, which proves my point about him adoring her. The way he leans in to listen to her, wraps his arm around her shoulders and regularly takes her hand and kisses it tells me all I need to know about their love. It will endure and stand the test of time; Edward is in this for keeps, and I hope Ava feels reassured now. She deserves to feel happy and to enjoy this time because life brings so many challenges that we need to grab happiness where and when we can. All we have is right here and now, this moment, and nothing else is guaranteed.

I carefully scan the room, making sure that glasses are filled, plates are cleared away, and no one goes without. It would help enormously to have a business partner to work alongside me at events like this, but it hasn't happened that way. Everything rests on my shoulders, but it's fine. It keeps me busy and means that I don't need to worry about anyone else messing up. It's all down to me.

My eyes wander over Jack's handsome face as he listens to Lucas. They're so alike in some ways and so different in others. Alike in that they have drive and ambition, they care for one another and for Edward, and different in that Jack has a hint of softness to him I haven't seen in Lucas. Maybe it's because I don't know Lucas well and haven't seen him in vulnerable moments like I've seen Jack. Having said that, earlier on, when I went out to the terrace, I saw Jack with another woman and my stomach knotted up at the way she gazed at him, the way she was pressing herself close to him and the way he seemed to let her. I've thought that he is tender and caring, but perhaps I was wrong. Perhaps it is all just about sex for him and he's more like my ex than I thought. Perhaps I attract a type, a breed of disloyal men driven by lust, men who want nothing more than to get their way and move to the next willing female target. If that's what Jack is really like, then ending things between us is wise and there should be no regrets. He's a playboy and I'm not on the market for heartache, however much I feel myself opening up to him in our intimate moments. Jack will probably go home with that woman tonight and fuck her on his sofa, and I'll be nothing more than a notch on his bedpost.

That thought smarts more than it should and I swallow hard, try to drag my eyes away from him, but it's like driving past a traffic accident. I feel the need to see what the outcome is even though looking at the scene hurts.

Will everyone be OK? Will there be survivors or will there be nothing but wreckage like the wreckage that's left of my foolish heart?

# Chapter 33

## *Jack*

'I can't believe it's my wedding day,' Edward says as I help him with his bow tie.

'Your second wedding day,' Lucas says, unnecessarily, and I shoot him a frown. 'Sorry ... me and my big feet.' He mimes putting his foot in his mouth.

'It's OK.' Edward looks in the mirror at the tie, then gives me a thumbs up. 'I'm feeling very positive about everything. Lucas is right ... this is my second wedding, but I'm OK with that. The first time was very different. I'm older and, I hope, wiser now and I'm doing this for the right reasons. Lucille was amazing in so many ways and marrying her was right at the time but obviously, things didn't work out and I've come to terms with that. Do I wish she was still around for Joe's sake? Of course I do and there's not much I wouldn't do to turn back time and stop her getting in that car, but sadly, I can't change what happened. However, Ava is incredible and I feel like the luckiest man in the world to be marrying her today.'

'You and Ava are good together,' I say, patting him on the back. 'You'll be very happy.'

'I think so too,' he says.

'You will,' Lucas joins us and gives Edward a hug. 'Cynical as I am, even I can see that. Ava is amazing and she'll be a wonderful wife to you.'

Edward nods, then looks across the bedroom to the window that overlooks the vast gardens. Joe is out there running around with his rescue greyhound, Kismet, and I see Edward's smile broaden. He loves Joe more than life itself and would do anything for him. From what I've seen of Ava, she cares for Joe too and will raise him as if he's her own.

'Perhaps we'll be able to give Joe some siblings, too.' Edward's cheeks colour slightly and I know he's thinking of Ava. 'It would be nice, but we'll have to wait and see. Marriage first then we'll take everything else one step at a time.'

'And I haven't even been married once,' Lucas says with a shrug.

'You've never wanted to get married,' I remind him.

'Why would I tie myself down to one woman when there's so many out there for me to try?' His grin is wolfish and makes me laugh, but Edward shakes his head.

'You'll find someone one day and she'll change your mind about playing the field. When you find the right woman, you'll give everything to be with her.'

Lucas and I both guffaw at this, and Edward scowls at us. Turning away to adjust my bow tie in the mirror, I wonder if

Edward's right. How do you know if you've met the right woman and how do you shake off the fear of committing to her? I thought I was there once and swore I'd never try again after how much being betrayed fucking hurt, but can I really keep on going like this for the rest of my life? It could be a long life if I'm lucky and I'll see my friends and brothers settling down. Will I always be alone? Will Lucas find his someone too and then it will be me who's the lonely bachelor? At the end of the day, if you don't have someone to go home to, it can be lonely. The question I have to ask myself is if being lonely is better than being fucking terrified of getting hurt?

'Right then,' Edward says, 'Shall we head downstairs?'

We go together, three friends who've been through a lot together. One of us is about to embark upon the next chapter of his life because he's far braver than I am. I'm happy for Edward but I can't help wishing that I could be in his shoes, but not with Ava, with the woman who recently has come to matter to me in ways I never thought possible.

## Chapter 34

### *Grace*

'That's it, Ava, smile for me!' Cindy Chong, the photographer, snaps away while Ava smiles uncertainly at the camera. I know this is hard for her because she's not a naturally outgoing person, but I smile encouragingly from behind Cindy and hope Ava will be able to relax a bit because today will involve a lot of posing for the camera. 'And can we have the mother of the bride, please?'

Nancy goes to stand with Ava, and I see the pride in her eyes. Ava is stunning in her beautiful champagne silk gown, the pearl tiara holding her long chestnut hair back from her face and the pearl studded veil in place. Nancy looks elegant in her outfit too. It takes me back to a similar day when I posed for photographs with Maisie and Riya. My mother was in my thoughts that day, my father too, and I hoped they could see me and that they were proud of me. I missed them so much, and still do, but when the day went so wrong, I was glad they weren't there to see my heart break. If it hadn't been for Maisie and Riya, I don't know how I'd have coped. They were the glue that held me together that day and got me home in one piece. Granted, they couldn't do my grieving for me, but they cared for me and I will be eternally grateful to them for being there.

'Right then,' I say, stepping in because I can see that Ava needs a breather. 'Shall we have a drink and a quick break before taking more photos?'

Cindy smiles at me, reading me well as we've worked together before and she says, 'I'll be back in fifteen. I'll catch up with the groom and some guests.'

'Thanks.' I flash her a smile and she leaves the bedroom.

'Thank you so much.' Ava shuffles over to the bed and sits down with a huff and her gown billows around her like a champagne cloud. 'I'm already exhausted.'

'Well, pace yourself because it's going to be a long day.' I grab a bottle of water from the dresser and pour some into a glass, then hand it to her. 'Stay hydrated. It will help.'

She accepts the glass gratefully and drinks, and I turn to Nancy. 'How're you feeling?'

I know Nancy has several conditions brought on by cancer treatment several years ago and that she needs to rest and stay hydrated, too.

'I'm very excited.' Nancy grins and I laugh.

'I'm glad.'

'I'll take some water, though.' She reaches for the bottle and fills a glass, then drinks long and deep. 'Mmmm. That's good.'

Crossing to the window, I watch as guests make their way to the large marquee in the garden. It's a beautiful sunny day, and the sky is flawless blue, the sun is shining and the air that enters through the open bedroom window is sweet with the scent of the roses that climb the trellis. Out on the grass, Joe, and his greyhound are running around and I see Ava's brother Daniel joining them. The dog jumps around excitedly and then does zoomies, making the boys laugh as they watch her. I can only hope that she doesn't knock someone over as they head for the marquee. All we need is for someone to have an accident so we need to call for an ambulance. But then I spot Jack and watch as he speaks to the boys and they both nod at him. Joe clips a lead to Kismet's harness and she stands at his side obediently. I send out a silent thank you to Jack for dealing with this in such a calm and sensible way.

Even from here I can see that he looks smart in his black suit with a white shirt and bow tie. His thick hair shines in the sunlight and I long to run my hands through it as I breathe him in. A powerful longing to touch him, to kiss his warm lips and to lose myself in him once more overwhelms me. It can't happen though, I know this, and yet knowing it doesn't stop the longing.

He crouches down and makes a fuss over the dog while talking to the boys. He's good with them and will one day make an amazing father, I'm sure. Some lucky woman will raise a family with him, a brood of babies that will have his gorgeous genes and ... *Stop it, Grace!*

Jack stands and looks up at the window, directly at me. I blush instantly but then realise he probably can't see inside because of the sun's glare on the glass. Regardless of that, I feel electricity flow between us like an invisible current that's always present whenever our eyes meet. Jack is a special guy and I wish things were different. Knowing he can't see me, I blow him a kiss, then turn from the window and brace myself to do my job on this glorious day.

# Chapter 35

## *Grace*

The day has been a success, the wedding ceremony was so beautiful and romantic that there wasn't a dry eye in the marquee, and now that the evening celebrations have begun I can relax a bit. Ava was the most beautiful bride I've ever seen, and she glowed all day, sparkled like a diamond, in fact, and her new husband has been glued to her side since she joined him at the end of the aisle. Her father attended the wedding, but it was her mother who walked her along the aisle. After what Ava told me about her past and how her father abandoned the family, it was fitting that her mum give her away, but nice that he made the effort to come and that he's trying to make up for what he did when she was younger. She told me she wanted her dad at the wedding, but that he's been absent from her life for so long that it's her mum she wanted to walk her down the aisle. Ava and Nancy are so close that I couldn't imagine it any other way. Before them, Joe walked with Kismet and the dog had a ring cushion attached to her collar, eliciting oohs and aaahs from the guests. Joe looked so proud that I had to clear the tears from my eyes more than once and when Edward saw Ava, I almost lost it. His face was just a perfect picture of love, and he even cried a few tears himself.

Throughout the ceremony, I kept my eyes away from Jack because I knew seeing him would be too much. I could sense him looking in my direction though, more than once, but I feigned interest in my iPad and in fussing around, making sure everything was running smoothly.

They cleared the aisle from the marquee to create the dance floor while everyone went out to the beautiful gardens for photographs, and then they served the food at the tables in the other half of the marquee. The food was delicious, the champagne flowed, and the speeches made everyone laugh and cry. Edward's speech was sweet and from the heart and Jack's made everyone smile while Lucas' was hilarious. The three men know one another so well they can get away with making fun of one another without causing offence. Although having said that, Lucas did mock himself more than he mocked Edward or Jack and I have to give him credit for that.

As dusk falls, I step outside for a moment to take some air. Fairy lights twinkle around the marquee and around the terrace. The air is filled with the sweetness of roses and the sharp freshness of the lavender and rosemary that grows in the stone pots. As music starts inside the marquee, the band that Edward booked for tonight, I lean against one of the marquee poles and close my eyes. I have enjoyed today, which fills me with hope because after everything, I'd lost the joy I once found in it. Seeing two people I like and care about get married has helped heal part of me and reminded me exactly what it is about this job that I love so much. One man took that from me and I never thought I'd get it back but it seems that time, and this wedding, have shown that I can move past what happened and rebuild my life, rebuild my happiness, find hope for the future. Seeing Ava and Edward today also gave me hope things could get better for me in that respect, too. Maybe I'll never find someone to look at me the way Edward looks at Ava, but that's OK because not everyone finds *the one*. Some of us just carry on alone, but we can still find joy in what life offers. I'm grateful to be alive on this beautiful planet and to have my health and my loved ones, to have the opportunities I do. There's happiness to be found in the simple things and going forwards I'm going to practise gratitude for what I do have rather than mourning what I don't.

'There you are.'

I open my eyes at the familiar voice and meet Jack's eyes.

'They're about to have the first dance, so I came to get you.'

'I needed some air,' I say.

'You've been very busy.' He holds out a hand. 'Coming?'

We haven't spoken all day and I've tried not to notice him, but it's been a struggle. It's like my eyes are drawn to him like metal to a magnet, and every time I've looked his way, my stomach has somersaulted.

I accept his hand, and when our skin meets, his pupils dilate.

'You gave them an incredible wedding, Grace. You're so amazing I find it hard to believe that you're real some days.'

'I did my job,' I say. My heart is thudding against my ribcage and I feel lightheaded.

'You're incredible at what you do.' He tugs my hand so I step closer to him. Gently, he places a finger under my chin and raises it so our eyes meet. There's something in his gaze that burns into me and I could scream with the intensity of it. 'You're incredible in every way, Grace.'

But not incredible enough that he wants to be with me…

'We'd better go inside,' I say as sadness washes over me.

The opening notes of the band's cover version of Ellie Goulding's beautiful song *How Long Will I Love You* drift out of the marquee. Jack holds my gaze for a moment longer then nods, and we head inside together to see Ava and Edward on the dance floor, the spotlight on them as they dance with eyes only for each other. Jack and I stand near the doorway still holding hands and watch as the bride and groom move around the dance floor together.

Soon I can't see a thing because of the tears in my eyes. And because of the ache in my heart at the knowledge that I have to let this lovely man go.

# Chapter 36

## *Jack*

Standing with Grace, I watch Edward holding his new bride close on the dance floor. It's a moving moment, even for a cynic like me. They move slowly to the romantic song, Ava's head on his chest, him resting his chin on her hair. When Ava looks up and their eyes meet, it's clear to everyone that they only have eyes for each other and that this is how it will be for the rest of their lives. How amazing to find a love like that, one that will last a lifetime. How rare...

As the song comes to an end, Edward kisses Ava and everyone claps and cheers. It has been an incredible day but a long one, in part because I've been near Grace all day but unable to hold her. There's a strange ache inside me because I'm longing to take her in my arms and I put it down to needing sex.

The band plays a cover of Gabrielle's *Under My Skin* next and guests take to the dance floor, surrounding Edward and Ava as they join the dancing. I look at Grace and see that she's nibbling at her lower lip. Does she want to dance too?

*Fuck it!*

I'm still holding her hand, so I lead her to the floor. She resists a bit at first, but I slide my arm around her waist and take her hand. She gazes up at me and I see doubt in her eyes so I lean forwards and whisper, 'I know you're working but you're allowed to dance, surely?'

She glances around us and sees everyone dancing and enjoying themselves and nods, so I pull her closer, ensuring that our bodies meet, feel her curves along my front in the way that makes me hard. Her pupils dilate as she feels my erection pressing into her and it takes everything I have to resist stealing a kiss.

When the song changes again and the band plays a cover of Sam Smith's *Too Good at Goodbyes,* I can't fight the need any longer and I whisper, 'Let's go outside.'

She barely nods in response before I march from the marquee with her right behind me. Outside, the evening air is cool, the gardens lit with fairy lights strung around the marquee and the rear of the grand house. A few people are milling around on the terrace, so I gesture at the land beyond the marquee and Grace pauses. Her chest is heaving and I see the outline of her nipples against the thin satin of her dress.

'Come with me,' I say.

'I can't. I'm ... working.'

'Grace ...' I take her hand again. 'Everyone's happy. Most people are drunk or on their way. You can relax now.'

I raise her hand and kiss it, turn it over and lick her palm and she gasps, then shivers with pleasure. I walk around her and stand behind her, pull her closer and kiss her neck from, nibble her ear lobes, push my erection against her bottom.

When she turns to face me, the desire in her eyes mirrors my own.

It is time ...

We head towards the darkness of the gardens, our breaths quick, our mutual need emerging from our mouths into the cool air.

We reach a copse of trees and I pull her behind them, then release her hand and remove my jacket. Grace turns away and looks back the way we came, as if debating whether to stay. Her curves are limned by the moonlight in all their glory, and my eyes are glued to her.

'You are the most beautiful thing I have ever seen and I'm obsessed with you,' I say, my voice gruff with desire and something else, something I don't want to admit to because it fucking terrifies me. 'Come to me, Grace.'

She turns to face me

Her lips part.

Her eyes are dark in her pale face.

What is she thinking?

And then ... She slips her dress from her shoulders and lets it fall to the ground. Standing there in a lacy, red strapless bra and tiny matching thong, she is positively Rubenesque and I know she will be my undoing.

My exhalation is a growl of passion and I reach for her, tug the bra down and fondle her exquisite breasts then take her nipples in my mouth in turn, run my tongue over the coffee stains of her areole, suck at the points and grin against her flesh as she moans.

There is darkness inside me and being with Grace like this unleashes it, makes me wild in ways I have tried to tame. It makes me want to taste her and so I push my hand under her thong and tear it from her, then scoop her up in my arms and lay her down on my jacket.

# Chapter 37

## *Grace*

I am naked outside and the air is cool on my exposed skin, but there's a fire burning inside me that radiates from my centre and warms me. Jack runs his hands all over my body, his touch electric, and I long for him to kiss me between my legs, but I also want this moment to last so I'm glad he doesn't rush.

When he straddles my legs, then pushes them apart, I wriggle in anticipation. I should have fought this, should have refused to come with him, but there's something in his eyes that tells me he wants this too, wants me as badly as I want him. Leading me outside like this at his best friend's wedding must mean something. His parents are in the marquee, his friends and acquaintances. Surely this means we are turning a corner and about to change our minds about what this is between us? I'm scared and yet I'm excited because I know now that I want more than goodbye from this wonderful man.

Jack kisses my thighs, his beard tickling my skin, then he

runs a finger over my sex and I gasp. The pressure building inside me is like a circuit that's about to overload.

He flicks his tongue over my clit and pushes two of his large fingers inside me at the same time, and then he works me the way only he knows how. As he fucks me with his mouth and stretches me with his fingers, I rise higher and higher, my whole body tense with need. But just as I'm about to come, he stops.

'Not yet, Goldie.'

He unzips his trousers and releases his cock and I see the bead of pre-cum at the tip, glistening in the moonlight like the promise of a diamond. He pulls a condom from his pocket and rolls it on, then hovers over me, rubs his cock over my clit, teases the already aroused bud.

'Take me, Jack.' I grip his hips and pull him inside me and he groans as he plunges deep.

We move together, my thighs around his, and we are frantic, desperate to reach the heights of desire together. Within seconds, I shudder as I tumble over the edge and he does too, emptying inside me, moving until we are both calm once more.

Still inside me, he gazes into my eyes and in the moonlight, I see the depths of emotion there. This man, he's different, he's special, he's everything I have ever wanted and the connection between us is undeniable.

'You are incredible,' he says. 'Only you could make me feel this way, Grace. There will never be anyone like you.'

He moves out of me, tidies himself up, then slips behind me and spoons me, his large body warming me, his arms wrapped around me like a large bear. Something has changed between us and we are at a new juncture in our relationship. I didn't expect this, but I am happy to embrace it because for me there is no one like Jack.

We stay that way for a while until we hear laughter across the gardens and then Jack helps me to dress, although my thong is torn so I have to go commando. He dangles the scrap of lace in front of me then presses it to his face and inhales and I feel desire sparkle inside me again.

'I'll keep this,' he says. 'A reminder of tonight.'

He tucks the thong into his jacket pocket, then slips the jacket around my shoulders and hugs me. I breathe him in, savour his warmth and how safe I feel in his arms.

I have no idea what happens now, but I'm looking forward to finding out.

## Chapter 38

*Jack*

We head back to the marquee and when we get there, Grace slips my jacket off her shoulders and hands it back to me. Her cheeks are pink and her eyes bright with what I can only describe as post-orgasm glow. Reaching out, I brush a lock of hair from her forehead, and she smiles.

Something in my chest shifts and it unsettles me. What was that? This woman is everything a man could want, everything I should want and yet ... Anxiety prickles at my edges because I cannot allow myself to feel this vulnerable. Right now, Grace is permeating the veneer I created around myself, getting closer to my heart and, to be frank, it fucking terrifies me.

'See you inside,' I say, then I turn and hurry into the marquee before I can allow myself to feel anything else. Maybe it was stupid of me to have sex with her again, but I couldn't resist. I needed to feel her warmth pulsing around my cock again, the sweetest, tight little pussy I know I'll never forget.

I needed to bury myself deep inside her.

*One last time...*

## Chapter 39

### *Grace*

Walking into the marquee, I can't stop smiling. What just happened outside with Jack was incredible. It's like I can't get enough of him. He's the sweetest addiction and I need to be with him like I need air and water.

I wander around the inner perimeter of the marquee, admiring the scene before me. The bride and groom are sitting at a table with family and Joe is sitting on Ava's lap, resting his head against her chest. They look so content, like the perfect little family, and my heart swells with joy for them. Everything will be OK for Ava from now on and she will have the best life. I hope we stay in touch because she has such a kind soul that she's the type of friend I want in my life.

The band plays and the evening wears on. More guests arrive to join the celebrations and the buffet is served. I lose track of time as I speak to guests and hand out my details to a few potential clients, something that makes me very happy indeed. Networking is crucial and there's nothing like an actual wedding to promote my business.

The band plays an old Gloria Estefan tune, *Rhythm Is Gonna Get You*, and I tap my feet. When Ava and some female guests head to the dance floor, I follow them and join their group. Everyone is smiling, dancing and having fun and I feel proud of what I've achieved here. I love my job and this wedding has helped to restore that for me.

We dance around, shaking our bottoms and waving our arms, and I'm laughing away when I spot Jack across the marquee. He's with an older couple and I realise they must be his parents. The man is almost as tall as Jack with white hair and moustache. He is handsome in that distinguished older man way and what some people would describe as a silver fox. Jack's mother looks smart in a pink dress and heels, her grey bob adorned with a feather fascinator. I can see both of them in Jack and my heart gives a little squeeze.

I'm wondering if I should go over to them to introduce myself when a younger woman joins them. Something sour rises in my throat as I witness the possessive way she places a hand on Jack's arm and steps in close. It's not helped by the fact that she looks a lot like Angelina Jolie with her long black hair, porcelain skin, incredible bone structure and wide smile. As I watch, Jack's parents greet her with hugs and kisses and Jack smiles at her in a way I'm sure he's never smiled at me. It's a smile of comfort and familiarity and when she throws her arms around his neck and laughs, my stomach plummets to the floor. The room spins and distorts and I'm catapulted back in time to a day when I knew my relationship was over, that I'd been misled and betrayed.

My chest tightens, my vision blurs, and I know I have to get out of there.

I hurry across the dance floor, blanking guests and serving staff, and exit the marquee with a gasp of dismay. Outside, I suck in the cool air as if it can ease my pain, and then I head for the house. Aware that I need to get myself together, that I have to be professional and accept that this is Jack's world, I try to calm myself down. This has always been Jack's world. It is not mine, as much as I might have dreamt that it could be.

Pausing at the open French doors that lead to the library, I gaze back at the marquee, and see Jack and the beautiful woman emerging together. As they head off across the lawns and disappear into the darkness, I know that whatever we had wasn't real. It was a distraction for him, a way to pass the time, and the reality is that he was always going to end up with a woman like that. Just like my fiancé. It seems they are all the same, after all.

# Chapter 40

## *Jack*

I knew Grace was watching. It was the quickest way to get the message across to her that it's over. It's not good for either of us to pursue things any more. What we had ended before it ever really began.

Lara made it easy, of course. She fawned all over me then when I suggested a stroll in the moonlight; she jumped at the chance. As we emerged from the marquee, I saw Grace standing near the house, her face hidden by shadows, but I knew what expression she would be wearing. One of sadness. I knew because it was how I felt as I led Lara away from the marquee — thoroughly wretched. It took all my strength not to leave Lara there and run over to Grace, to grab her and pull her close to me and never let her go. But what would that achieve? Sooner or later, one of us would get hurt because I am damaged, and the longer it goes on between us, the harder it will be to end things. Grace needs a man who can give her everything she desires and deserves, and I'm simply too broken for that. Once upon a time, I was whole, but then Lara showed me how easily I could be destroyed and it will never happen again. I wouldn't survive a second time.

As we walked away from the marquee and across the lawns, I forced fake laughter from my mouth, but my heart ached for Grace and for what we had shared. The sex was incredible, but there was something more there and that was what fucking terrified me the most.

When we reached the stone steps that led down to the next level of the garden, I paused at the bottom and Lara turned to me, placed a hand over my heart and gazed up at me expectantly. I could see in her eyes that she wanted me, that she wanted to feel the way she used to do when we were together. All the emotions I'd felt since I discovered her cheating on me surged like a tidal wave, and I trembled from head to toe, a quivering wreck of the man I tried to be. The man I wanted to be. The man I lost when I was betrayed.

Lara stepped closer, and I felt her press herself along the front of me — taller than Grace, slimmer than Grace, wearing a different perfume to Grace.

And then it hit me.

She was not Grace.

She could not compare to Grace.

There never will be anyone like Grace for me again.

I am ruined…

# Chapter 41

## *Grace*

Six weeks later, I am sitting in the café at my usual table. June has been hot in the city and the door to the café is open, the rainbow bead curtain in the doorway swaying slightly in the gentle breeze. My laptop is open, a spreadsheet of numbers on the screen. This is my least favourite part of owning my own business, but it has to be done as I have a meeting with my accountant this week and need everything up to date for her to go through.

The sunshine on the glass is making me sleepy and I'm tempted to close the laptop and go for a walk, maybe head to a park where I can relax in a green space and let my thoughts wander. I will not lie; the past six weeks have been bumpy. There's been a lot of reflection, some self-recrimination and a significant amount of tears. After the wedding, I blocked Jack's number and email and made myself take a social media break except with my business accounts, which I had to keep running because I can't afford to lose potential clients over a man again. Poor Maisie and Riya were worried, but they understood why I was upset and so they held me, mopped up my tears and told me everything would be all right in the end.

And I believe them.

Last time, I didn't because it was all so hard, but this time I've lost a fuck buddy, not a fiancé and that has to be easier to get over, surely? We had no shared possessions or plans and when I actually thought about what we'd agreed at the start of our fling, I could rationalise that we would never be more than temporary. For some stupid reason, I allowed myself to get carried away with romantic fantasies about where our relationship was going and it was ridiculous because we come from different worlds. Jack told me from the start that he had baggage and could offer me nothing permanent and I told him the same. I wasn't lying and the way I've felt since the wedding is proof of that. I still had issues to work through from my past and was not in a good place to start something new with Jack. Besides which, the prospect of competing with women like the Angelina Jolie lookalike to try to hold Jack's interest is a headache I do not need. Not now and not ever. I'm going to focus on my business and my life and building something no man can ever take away from me.

The beads at the doorway rattle and I look up to see a familiar face.

'Hey there.' Ava comes to my table, her face lit up by her beautiful smile.

'Hello.' Standing, I open my arms and hug her, then step back and look at her. 'Well, my lovely, marriage suits you.'

'Thank you. Am I OK to join you?' She gestures at the table.

'Of course. Would you like something to drink?'

She glances at the menu on a board above the counter and nods. 'An iced tea would be wonderful, thanks.'

I ask Maisie for two iced teas, then return to Ava.

'How have you been?' I ask as I sit back down and close my laptop because I have a good excuse now.

'Really well.' She pushes her hair back from her cheeks and waves a hand. 'It's warm, isn't it?'

'Very.'

She hangs her bag on the back of her chair, then leans forwards and folds her hands on the table in front of her. 'How are you?'

Her pretty amber eyes scan my face and I smile, but I can see concern in her gaze and I know then that she knows something of what happened with Jack.

'I'm good, thanks. Busy.'

'That's good to hear, Grace. Thank you,' she says to Maisie as she sets two glasses of iced tea on the table along with a plate of lemon snaps.

'You're welcome. Let me know if I can get you anything else.' Maisie smiles at us both, then heads back to the counter.

'How was your honeymoon?' I ask.

'Incredible. Let me bore you with some photos.' Ava gets her phone out of her bag and flicks through some photographs, and I can see how amazing it was. Along with Edward and Joe, she smiles and poses at some of Italy's most beautiful spots with lakes, mountains, and vineyards behind them.

'It looks like you had a magical time.'

'We did. The month flew past and since we got home, we've been busy sending out thank you cards, visiting friends and family and I've done a few days with the dog rescue charity. I honestly can't believe how quickly time goes but I have been meaning to visit you.'

'You have?'

She nods then takes a sip of her drink. 'Well, we're friends, aren't we?'

'I'd like to think so.'

'I've been worried about you, Grace.'

'Me? But why?'

'You and Jack ... that didn't end well?'

'Me and Jack?'

The slight rise of her eyebrows tells me I don't need to pretend, so I sigh and rest my elbows on the table. 'It wasn't ever going to go anywhere.' The ice in my drink clinks and a bead of condensation runs down the glass and pools on the table. 'And it was unprofessional of me to get involved with him anyway and for that, I'm really sorry.'

'Why was it unprofessional?' she asks.

'I was working and should never have entertained the idea of seeing the friend of a client.'

'Grace, Edward and I had no problem with that. Initially, Edward was a bit concerned because he knows what Jack has been through in the past and he was worried about Jack getting hurt, but he was also worried about you being hurt if Jack didn't act appropriately towards you. Jack has developed a bit of a reputation as a playboy, but Edward told me it's a more recent thing. An ex hurt him, and it hardened him, but then you came along and he seemed to change. I honestly think he really liked you.'

*Liked.*

'We don't think that meeting someone and spending time with them is unprofessional at all.' She sips her drink then wipes her hands on a napkin. 'You're allowed to be happy, you know.'

I swallow hard. She's caught me off guard, and I don't know how to respond. 'I ... I liked Jack a lot, but it was going nowhere. I have baggage too and we're just very different.'

'In what way?' She tilts her head.

'Well ... we come from different worlds.'

'Do you?'

I laugh then. 'I'm a struggling business owner and he's an incredibly rich executive. He has money to burn, but I'm looking at my bottom line and wondering how I'm ever going to get out of the red.'

'That's just money.' She waves a hand. 'Don't get me wrong. I've been there. I was broke before I got the job as Joe's nanny and it truly changed my life. But I would have fallen in love with Edward if he'd had nothing. I found the wealth overwhelming at first and to be honest, I still do, but it's just a part of our life. Edward is an incredible man and I would love him even if he lost it all tomorrow. What matters is the connection you have with someone.'

'Ava ... thank you ... but it's not just the money and the circles we move in. My ex hurt me too and some days I struggle to deal with that. I swore I'd never get involved again and Jack was a ... a mistake. I don't have the time or energy for love.'

Nodding slowly, she reaches over the table and squeezes my hand. 'I understand. I know what it's like to be afraid, albeit for different reasons. But I think you should know that Jack has been struggling since the wedding.'

'Jack? But why?'

'He might have a tough exterior, but it's fragile as a shell and it's cracking. I saw you together and I saw the way he looked at you and I'm convinced he really liked you. More than liked you, I'd say by the way he's been since. We went away on honeymoon and when we came home, Edward went to see him and said he was lower than ever. Grace, I think he's afraid, and now I know that you are too. But if that's all that's stopping you being together, then there must be a way to sort this out.'

The thought that Jack is low saddens me and yet it cheers me because he must have cared about me. Is he as conflicted as I am about everything, then?

'What about Angelina Jolie?' I ask, my stomach turning at the thought of that beautiful woman at the wedding.

'Who?' Ava frowns.

'The gorgeous woman at the wedding. Long black hair, figure to die for. Incredible bone structure.' I tap my own cheeks, conscious of the lack of razor sculpted cheekbones.

'Oh, you mean Lara,' she replies.

'Lara.' The name rolls off my tongue, leaving a sour taste.

'She's Jack's ex. She cheated on him when they were together and really messed him up. There's nothing between them now, though. Jack's polite to her because their mothers are best friends, but he'd never go back to her. That ship has sailed.'

'Really?'

'Absolutely. Lara is still with the guy she cheated on Jack with. Between us, I think she would love to have Jack back, but he's not interested.'

'I see.' *He's not with her! He's not interested.* I want to punch the air. Of course, I don't, but my hands ball into fists under the table anyway and I bump them together just to ease the desire to celebrate.

'Why don't you call him? Perhaps get together and talk?'

'I blocked his number.'

'I know. He told Edward that he couldn't get through to you.'

'He could have called from a different number,' I say pedantically.

'He felt that if you'd done that, you wouldn't want to hear from him. I think Jack is stubborn and, no offence, Grace, but you are too.'

That makes me snort and I shake my head. 'Yeah, I've heard that before.'

'So will you consider calling him?'

'I'll think about it.' I take a sip of my drink, savouring the cold, refreshing tea as it slides down my throat.

'Anyway … that wasn't all I wanted to speak to you about,' she says.

'No?'

'I have a proposition for you. A business proposition.'

'You do?'

Her grin intrigues me, and I sit forwards to listen carefully.

'As a wedding present, Edward gave me some money. It's a large sum, and I tried to decline it but he wouldn't hear of it. He knows I want to work too and while I help out with the dog rescue charity, I'd like something more.'

'Something for you,' I say.

'Exactly that.' Nodding, she licks her lips. 'I loved our wedding and the whole experience of it. I found your role fascinating and realised I'd love to work with you.'

'With me?'

'Yes. Look, there's no pressure, but how would you feel about me investing in your business?'

'In my business?' My voice is a squeak.

'Sorry.' She places a hand on her chest. 'You hate the idea. It's no problem at all. Forget I mentioned it.'

'No! Please, no! Ava ... this is ... just wow. You want to invest in my business?'

'I do. But I'd also like to work with you. If you'd be happy for me to do so.'

'You want to invest in my business and to work with me? As a partner?'

'I would love that. I know little about it all, but if you'd be happy to teach me, I'd love to learn.'

'Oh my god! I would love that!'

She wants to invest in my business and to work with me. I wouldn't be alone anymore and I'd have help and a friend and partner. A weight I've been carrying around for months suddenly lifts from my shoulders as relief floods through me.

'You would?' she asks.

'Yes!' I stand up, lean over and hug her, swaying from side to side with excitement, and she laughs.

'I'm so happy.'

'Me too.'

And I am. Yes, there will be paperwork to sign and legalities to sort out, but it's nothing that can't be done

'How do you fancy going office hunting?' she asks. 'It's lovely here, but if there are two of us, I think we could do with having a proper office space.'

'I would love that.'

'Well, let's go then,' she says, standing too.

I tell Maisie where I'm going and she grins at me, then I grab my bag and head out into the beautiful June sunshine with my new business partner. Life isn't easy, but people can make it more bearable and Ava Cavendish is one of those people. Right now, I'm so grateful I could burst. Pulling my phone from my bag, I scroll to blocked numbers and unblock Jack. I won't call him yet because I need to think about things in light of what Ava's told me, but it's a step in that direction and, I hope, a positive one.

## Chapter 42
### *Grace*

It takes us nearly three months to find the right office and to process all the paperwork, but now here we are as business partners. We've hired an official photographer for the evening because we want to use the photographs for our website. I'm so excited I could burst and from the glow in her cheeks, and the way Ava has bounced around the office on Salem Road all day, I'd say she's excited too. It's a short walk to Cupcake Corner, and seeing as how I'm still living above the café for now, that's a definite advantage. The office rent isn't cheap but we've got a few bookings over the coming months for some of Edward's friends and colleagues, so we're confident we'll make enough to cover the rent and attract similar clientele who'll want our premium packages.

'Isn't this fancy?' Maisie and Riya have arrived, and they're gazing around the ground floor space in awe. I don't blame them because I did the same when I first came here. From the flawless finish to the sanded floorboards, circular lights, and sash windows with their dove grey frames, the office is stylish. It says bespoke weddings will be planned here by creative professionals. There's a kitchenette out back, a small courtyard and even a wet room.

'I'm glad you think so,' I reply. I told them to wait until we had our official opening to see the office because Ava and I wanted our furniture in first and I'm glad because now they get to see it properly. Ava has an amazing eye for interior décor and, from what I've seen so far, she also knows her way around a wedding dress. It's so much fun having a partner I can trust to work alongside me and I'm enjoying having someone else to consult about things. I might even get a holiday in this year because I know I can leave the business in Ava's capable hands.

'You're going to be a roaring success,' Riya says.

'I hope so.'

'Grace, shall we reveal the name now?' Ava says from across the office. She's standing near the front window that overlooks the street. A roll of paper covers the glass because we wanted to reveal the name this evening.

'Yes!' I smiled at my aunt and her partner, then skip over to Ava and accept the glass of champagne she offers me.

We all file outside and stand in front of the window.

'This evening we are here to celebrate our union,' Ava says with a giggle. 'As business partners.' She wraps her free arm around my shoulders and I slide my arm around her waist.

'Thank you for coming to share in this with us.' I smile at our friends and family who have gathered here to help us celebrate. They smile back, from Edward and Nancy, to

*Healing the Billionaire's Heart*

Toni and Freddy, to Lucas and his latest lady friend and others.

For a moment, as I gaze at them all, I feel a surge of sadness for the one man who isn't here. Ava said we should probably invite him and so I swallowed my pride and sent him a text message last week, but he didn't reply. I don't blame him. It's been a while since the wedding and despite what Ava said, I'm sure he's happy again with Lara, although Ava has insisted that this isn't true. I could have messaged him sooner, but I've been busy, or so that's what I kept telling myself. Work, and setting up as business partners with Ava has kept me busy, but I've also been doing things for me. I started swimming at a nearby lido in the mornings and I find it sets me up nicely for the day. At first, I was apprehensive about going there, but after the first few times — when I saw that people of all shapes and sizes swim there and don't care about donning swimwear in public — I stopped caring too. I've even been chatted up a few times at the poolside, but I'm simply not interested and so the men in question soon move on. It was nice to have a confidence boost, but I know I'm still too fond of Jack to look at another man.

'And without further ado...' Ava says as we turn to the window and she takes hold of one end of the paper and I grab the other. 'Welcome to ... *Amazing Grace Weddings*!'

The paper falls away and the gold calligraphy is revealed on the glass. The name was Ava's suggestion. We spent some time playing around with both our names but Ava said she loved this one and I have to admit, so do I.

Our guests clap and cheer and the servers pop champagne corks and top up glasses. Edward comes to Ava, takes her in his arms and kisses her in the way I know makes her knees weak. As they all go back inside, I stand alone and gaze at the window. Through the glass I can see smiling faces, people celebrating and enjoying the moment, and it warms my heart.

'Congratulations.' A deep voice behind me sends a shiver down my spine and my body reacts despite my brain telling it not to. 'It looks amazing, Grace.'

Turning, I look up into Jack's beautiful eyes. 'I see what you did there,' I reply, and he laughs. 'I didn't think you were going to come.'

'What? And miss this?' He gestures at the office behind me. 'I wouldn't miss it for the world, Goldie.'

We stand there, eyes locked, bodies centimetres apart, hearts racing.

*What now?* I want to ask but don't because I'm scared.

'Can we talk?' he says. 'In private?'

I nod. 'There's a courtyard out the back. We can go there.'

I head back inside, and he follows me. My chest is so tight I can barely breathe and my mouth has gone dry but my brain is screaming out: *Jack has come! He cares, and that's why he has come!*

We reach the back door and exit through it, and Jack closes it behind us.

We are alone again.

At last.

# Chapter 13

## *Jack*

I follow Grace through the office, smiling at a few people who catch my eye, and out through the door at the back. Grace is breath-taking this evening in a white silk dress that sits just above her knees and has floaty sleeves that fall to her elbows. I noticed Ava was also wearing white, so guess it's their nod to all things bridal. Grace wears white well and her long blonde hair tumbles over her shoulders in sexy shiny waves. It makes me want to wind my hands in it and tilt her head so I can kiss those pretty lips of hers. I have missed kissing her. Badly. But I've also been trying to work through my issues and to get myself to a place where I can embrace love again.

Outside, the air is mild and fragranced with the sweetness of the honeysuckle that climbs from a planter in the courtyard and drapes itself over the fence. The mornings already whisper of autumn now, but the evenings still cling to late summer as if it refusing to let go yet.

Grace pulls out a wicker chair at a table and sits down, perched on the end as if preparing to leave should the need arise. I sit too, then shuffle my chair closer to hers. What I need to say requires proximity to this woman.

'How have you been?' I ask, scanning her face.

'Good.' She gives a small nod. 'Busy.'

'So I've heard.'

'Oh?' She tilts her head.

'From Edward.'

'He's been reporting back, has he?' She raises a brow, then a hint of a smile plays on her lips.

'No. Not like that. But I have asked after you and he's told me about you and Ava setting up in business together and how well it's been going. When you messaged me, I wanted to reply, but I was afraid. I thought I'd wait and come this evening to see you instead because there's too much that can be misunderstood in a text message.'

'Did you think you might not come?' Her eyes are filled with emotion, and I struggle to resist reaching out and stroking her cheek.

I don't want to lie, so I incline my head. 'I thought about it a lot. The last thing I wanted was to ruin this evening for you or to tarnish the memory of it. It's a special celebration and you and Ava both deserve to enjoy it.'

'Thank you.' She smiles.

'What for?'

'Being considerate of our feelings. But ... you came.'

A statement, not a question.

'I came. I wanted ... needed to see you.'

'Now you've seen me.' Her lips curves upwards and I see a teasing glint in her eyes. 'What do you think, Bear?'

'I think you're more beautiful than ever, Goldie.'

'It's all the porridge I've been eating after my morning swims.'

'You've been swimming?'

She nods. 'I'm getting quite good at it, actually. I never thought I'd enjoy it because my main experience of swimming was at school when ... when people poked fun at me because of my figure.' She bites her lower lip as if the memory distresses her. 'But the people at the lido don't care. They're there to swim and enjoy themselves and it's helped me to let go.'

'Your figure is incredible, Grace, and you should never hide it away. I love your body.' An image of her naked flashes before me and my cock twitches. It makes me sad she doesn't realise exactly how fucking gorgeous she is.

She looks down at her hands that are folded in her lap and I notice her nails are painted with a pearly varnish to match her dress. The small details like that are what get to me when I'm with her. She's sweet and caring and beautiful and she's got to me like no one ever has done before. Not even Lara.

'Grace,' I rest my elbows on my knees as I lean forwards. 'If I hurt you, I'm sorry. I never meant to cause you pain.'

She shrugs. 'We never made any promises to each other,

except at the start when we agreed that we'd see things as temporary.'

'I'm in business,' I say, holding my hands out, palms facing upwards. 'When I make an agreement, I stick to it. Usually, it also involves shaking hands and signing on the dotted line. We didn't have a contract, but it felt like it.'

'We had an oral contract, didn't we?' She licks her lips and for a minute all I can think about is oral with her, me tasting that sweet pussy, her sucking my cock, our bodies fitting together in the way it seems they were made to do. 'I didn't expect more from you.'

'But I think we both found ourselves wanting more.' She doesn't deny it, so I go on. 'I got scared, Grace. Fucking terrified, in fact. You got under my skin and I didn't know how to deal with that.'

She sighs and pushes her long hair behind her small ears and I see the pearls in her lobes, as perfect and pure as she is.

'I told you I have baggage and I do.' I clear my throat. 'See ... Lara and I ... we were very young when we got together. I adored her, and I thought that was it, that we'd get married, have children and live happily ever after. It was comfortable, and I thought I had no reason not to trust her, but it turned out that I shouldn't have believed in her or in us. I used to spend my time with her and with a friend, Maxwell, someone I'd known since primary school. The three of us were friends through school and then when we got to sixth form, Lara and I became an item. I knew Maxwell liked her too, but I was young and horny and well ... you've seen Lara.'

'I have.' Grace presses her lips together until they turn white.

'She's stunning, but I don't see her in that way any longer.'

'You left the wedding party together.' Her tone is laced with bitterness and I don't blame her.

'I did, but we walked for a bit and ... and nothing happened.'

'Would she have liked something to happen?' Grace sits up straight and lifts her little chin.

'She would. But I'd never go there again. She's not the person I thought she was. I don't find her attractive now and haven't for a long time.'

'Really?'

'I promise.' Nodding vigorously, I hope she believes me. 'When I was with her ... We all went off to university, but while I went to Oxford, they went to Bath. They were friends, I told myself, when they'd send me messages about studying together, going to clubs and so on. I trusted them both. Until I didn't.'

'What happened?'

It wasn't until a few years ago when Lara and I were living together that I found out there was more to their relationship. Maxwell had been travelling after working for a year in Australia and he came to London, and rather than him pay for a hotel, we said he could crash at our place.

'One night...' My jaw tenses, and I rub it to try to ease the tension. 'One night I had a late meeting and I messaged Lara to say I'd be home around ten. However, I got home earlier than that. I ... let myself in and went straight to the bedroom to change because I was sick of wearing a suit and that was when I-I found them.'

'Lara and Maxwell?' Grace asks.

I nod. Rub my eyes to get rid of the image of a naked Lara on all fours in front of Maxwell while he thrust into her from behind. She was putting on a full show the way she did with me in the early days, and I stood there, frozen to the spot as my best friend emptied his balls inside my girlfriend.

'It was only after they'd finished that they noticed me,' I whisper.

'Oh shit, Jack, I'm so sorry.' Grace shakes her head. 'That's awful.'

'I told them both to get the fuck out, and they did. Lara begged me to forgive her, but I told her she was dead to me.'

'That kind of betrayal takes time to recover from. If you ever do.' Grace's eyes are shining.

'I didn't think I ever would. It was some time ago, obviously, but it's been like a scar etched on my heart and I never thought it would heal, but then I met you.'

Grace's eyes widen. 'What do you mean?'

'You helped me to heal. It didn't happen overnight but being with you, holding you and laughing with you have helped me. Grace, *you* have helped me to move past what happened and finally I feel ready to move on.'

'You do?'

'Yes. But I want to move on with you. I have missed you so much the past few months and I know now that my feelings for you are real and that they'll last.'

I move closer to take her hand, to ask her what I need to ask her, but she shakes her head. 'This is a lot, Jack. I-I have baggage too. It's why I didn't cope too well when you rejected me.'

'I didn't reject you.'

'Maybe not directly, but it was there nonetheless. I could feel myself growing fond of you, and at the wedding, after we'd made love, I thought it was a sign that things were going somewhere between us and then ...'

'You saw me with Lara.'

'Yes.'

'I'm so sorry that I got scared. I knew I was falling for you and it terrified me.'

'Me too.' She stares at me, her eyes momentarily hard, but then they soften again.

'What happened to you, Grace? Can you tell me?'

She takes a deep breath, and then she meets my eyes again. 'I was in love once, too.'

# Chapter 44

## *Grace*

'His name was Walton Devoe.' I let the name roll off my tongue, waiting for the jolt of pain but it doesn't come and I'm relieved.

'The app creator?' Jack's brows meet.

'That's the one.' I nod. 'He made his fortune from designing apps to help with mood and anxiety, something I think is ironic considering the anxiety and low mood he caused me. He also designed an app to help university students to organise their time better, based on how he managed as a student himself. As far as I know, he's still designing others and has increased his wealth by selling some of his ideas, too.' Waving my hand, I try to show Jack that I no longer care about what Walton does.

'I'm sorry,' Jack says.

'It's not your fault.'

'I'm sorry that he hurt you. What happened, exactly?'

'He jilted me at the altar.'

'What?' Jack's eyes widen.

'I know. How humiliating for me, a wedding planner, to be jilted on my wedding day, right?' Heat rushes into my cheeks at the memory of that awful day four years ago. 'We'd booked a beautiful hotel in Scotland on the edge of a loch. Our family and friends came the day before to stay there and at the surrounding lodges, also owned by the hotel. It seemed so perfect when I rose that morning, my heart full of hope. I walked along the side of the loch, watching as the mist gently dispersed and the sun rose in the sky. It was such a peaceful place, and I thought I was at the start of a beautiful adventure. Turned out I was at the end of my relationship, but apparently it had already been over for some time and I was none the wiser.' A wry laugh escapes my lips and I rub my mouth, keen to remove the tarnish left by Walton. I don't say this out loud but my ex fiancé now belongs to a strawberry blonde haired impossibly leggy twenty-three-year-old social media influencer called Beatrix *bitch-face* Bamford-Higgs. OK, so *bitch-face* was just something I added to the mix because I was smarting from the fact that she walked into my life, kicked me out of it and stole my fiancé, but still... Calling her the odd name helped with my healing process, or so I used to tell myself. Don't get me wrong, I was bloody furious with him too. Walton *bastard-face superstar businessman and self-made multimillionaire* Devoe, became my least favourite person on this earth. It often strikes me how funny it is (funny, strange, not funny ha ha) that a person you once loved and adored can become the person you hate from the depths of your now dark and wounded soul.

'Don't tell me he went through with it?' Jack asks.

'Oh no ... but almost.' My mind drifts back to that morning as I dressed and had my hair and makeup done. Maisie took me aside and told me that if I wasn't certain then I shouldn't go ahead with it. I wasn't sure why because she knew I loved him, but there was something in her eyes that told me more than her words did. She knew it wasn't right, but she wasn't about to interfere because she believed it should be my decision. 'I descended the staircase carefully in my long white gown, my aunt Maisie at my side, and reached the doorway to the room that overlooked the loch. The guests fell silent and then the harpist began to play. We walked into the room and all eyes moved our way. It was hard for me because I'm not keen on being the centre of attention, but Walton had insisted on having a big wedding. I met his eyes across the room and saw not love but panic in them, the way he rubbed a finger under his collar and, as I got closer, the sheen of sweat on his brow. And then ... when I reached him and handed Maisie my bouquet, I went to take his hand but he ... he...' Now I suck in a breath because the memory is so vivid it makes my chest as tight as if I'm being crushed by a bower constrictor. 'He shook his head and ... and ran.'

'He ran?' Jack asks incredulously.

'He ran. Along the aisle, out of the doors and from the hotel.'

'What a shithead.' Jack's cheeks redden with anger. 'That's an awful thing to do to you.'

I shrug. 'Yeah. Maybe. But he clearly didn't really want to marry me. Oh it was terrible, Jack, at the time. I was utterly humiliated and broke down there and then. For days I was inconsolable, kept thinking he'd come back and apologise and we'd sort it out. As a wedding planner, I know people get nervous and sometimes need more time. The thought that he'd just run away seemed implausible, so I expected him to return and ask me to forgive him.'

'I take it he didn't?' Jack rubs at his cheeks.

'He didn't. Instead, he sent me a text message to tell me it had all been a big mistake and that he was in love with a colleague who'd been working on his latest app with him. All the nights I thought he was working and in meetings, he'd actually been with her. She was, of course, younger, fitter, and far more beautiful than me, and he'd grown fond of her, he said. The worst thing was that she was at our wedding, sitting on his side of the aisle, watching all this unfold. She left too, right after him, and they went on our honeymoon to Thailand.'

'Wow.' Jack stands up and paces up and down the courtyard. 'I know it probably doesn't feel like it, but you had a lucky escape.'

Standing too, I laugh. 'Oh, believe me, it does. I definitely had a lucky escape. We could have been married and then I'd have been even more committed.'

'It's taken you time to move on?' he asks.

'Well, I lost my mind for a bit because I was broken by what had happened and I struggled to work because how could I plan magnificent weddings when my own had gone so wrong? And then, unfortunately, lockdown hit and I lost everything. Without weddings to plan, I couldn't pay the rent on my office or the apartment I'd shared with Walton, which was insanely expensive but I'd always insisted on paying my half, and so I had to give both up and move in with my aunt and Riya. That's why I ended up working from home, or mainly from their café, and why I've still been trying to get on top of everything again.'

'It's been a hard time for so many people,' Jack says. 'We had a bit of a rocky time at Cavendish Construction but as we emerged from lockdown, the demand for construction was at a high and so we've clawed our way back. Of course, Edward was also going through his own difficulties back then, but thankfully that's in the past and we're all moving forwards now.' He smiles. 'And it looks like your business is on the up now, too.'

Smiling back, I nod. 'Thank goodness! I have the best partner now and this gorgeous new office and I'm feeling so much better than I did.'

Jack walks slowly towards me and takes my hands. His feel so big as they enfold mine and his touch sends fire to my core.

'Have you seen Walton since?'

Nodding, I say, 'I saw him once at a function in London about a year ago and he was with her. It was hard but also good for me to have closure. I don't know if he ever loved me, but I don't think he could have because when you love someone, you just don't treat them like that. It's why I have a major problem with cheating.'

'Me too. There's no room for it in my life.'

'But what about all the women you've been with since Lara?' The thought is like a knife through my heart, but I have to ask.

'They didn't mean anything and I never cheated on them. It was always made clear that I didn't want anything more than sex.' When he sees me wince, he touches my cheek gently. 'It was a physical function, a way of telling myself that I didn't want more, that I would never need more. Until now.'

His brown eyes hold mine captive.

'Until now?'

'Now, Grace, I can't imagine not wanting more. But only with you.'

'With me?'

He smiles. 'Of course with you. Grace, I've fallen hard for you. When I didn't see you, it was hell. The thought that you might never want to be with me again drove me crazy, and it's been so difficult not banging on your door and begging you to be mine.'

'It has?'

He laughs. 'Are you going to respond to everything I say with questions?'

'Am I?' I tease, and he laughs again.

'How do you feel about me, Grace?'

Chewing my bottom lip, I look down and think before meeting his gaze again. 'That depends.'

'On what?'

'On what you want from me.'

'I want you, Grace. I want to be with you every day for the rest of my life.'

'What?' Blinking rapidly, I drag air into my lungs.

'I love you. Please be mine for the rest of our lives. I don't want to waste another minute being sad.'

A beat of silence hovers between us and electricity crackles in the air. He wants me to be his. Always.

'I–I can't do the whole big wedding thing, though.'

'Is that a yes, then?'

'A yes to what?' My mind is whirling like a cauldron of confusion and I feel slow, like I can't really absorb what I'm being told.

'Grace, I love you and I know we haven't known each other long, but I'm done with playing around. I'm done with being away from you. I know I want you and that I'll never want another. We've both been hurt, but I promise you that if you agree to be my wife, I will stay faithful to you for the rest of my days. I will strive to make you happy. I will give you the world.'

'Oh, my god.' My mouth falls open as he drops to one knee and takes my left hand, presses a kiss to my fingers. 'You're proposing?'

'It looks that way, yes.' He rests his forehead against my fingers, and I feel him shaking with laughter. 'It's not going quite as romantically as I'd envisaged, but hey, who's judging us, right?'

I laugh too, but stop when he pulls a ring from his pocket. It's a red gold band adorned with white gold leaves and with a large square diamond at the centre.

'OK then ...' He takes a deep breath. 'Grace Cosgrove, I have adored you since the moment we met and I love you with everything I have to give. Will you marry me so we can be together forever?'

'On one condition,' I say, amazed at my bravery.

He looks up, a query in his eyes.

'No big wedding,' I say, and he nods.

'Grace Cosgrove,' he says again, 'Will you run away to Vegas with me to get married?'

'I will!'

He slides the ring onto my finger, then stands up and takes my face in his hands. He holds my gaze before lowering his head and kissing me.

His lips are soft and warm, his tongue gently pushes between my lips and then tangles with mine. All the passion and sadness that have built up in me since I saw him at Ava and Edward's wedding surge upwards and I kiss him back like I never want to stop.

He shuffles us backwards and sits down, then pulls me onto his lap. Straddling him there on the chair in the courtyard, I know I've got to have him.

I push my thong aside and he frees his cock, pulls out a condom, and then he meets my gaze as he rolls it on.

'Grace, I love you.'

I rise above his lap then lower onto his hard length, throw back my head as he fills me, touching me inside in ways only he ever has done. Physically. Emotionally. Eternally.

At first we move together slowly, his hands gripping my hips firmly as he controls us, but soon our desire rises and we speed up. He moves a hand down and places the pad of the thumb on my clit and I climb towards the peak of pleasure then we tumble over the edge together and I cry out his name over and over again.

'I love you, Jack,' I say when we are still once more.

'I loved you before we even met, Grace. I was just waiting for you to arrive.'

He holds me close and I rest my head in the crook of his shoulder, breathing him in, feeling safe and loved. I know that Jack will never hurt me. He will always have my back as I will have his.

# Epilogue - Grace

'Vegas is great,' I say as I stretch out in the king-size bed of the penthouse suite in the Bellagio Hotel. The opulent suite is decorated in shades of violet and bronze, has marble everywhere, and could house several families easily. It has an enormous bath, large shower room, walk in wardrobes and floor to ceiling windows with incredible views of Vegas. It's luxurious and beautiful and I'm here with Jack and having the best time.

'How would you know?' Jack asks with a laugh. 'You've spent most of it in bed.' He tickles me under my ribs and I giggle because he's right.

Since we arrived in Las Vegas a week ago, we've enjoyed this suite immensely. Well, we've enjoyed each other in this suite immensely. I'm still amazed by how strong our desire is. It's been a year since Ava and Edward's wedding and although we had planned to jet off sooner, Ava and I have been incredibly busy with our business and even had to employ two assistants to help us stay on top of it all. It meant that Jack and I had to wait a bit longer, but it has

## Epilogue - Grace

been worth it. We married yesterday in the Graceland Chapel, had two strangers as witnesses, and took photographs with our phones. I wore a navy satin dress and strappy sandals and carried a bouquet of white roses and Jack wore a navy suit and a white shirt. I had Maisie and Riya on FaceTime on my phone and Jack had his family on his so they could watch us marry. We walked down the aisle together and held hands throughout. There was no stress, no worry and no anxiety and it was, I have to say, the happiest day of my life. It was all about Jack and me and no one else. I did feel I was betraying my commitment to my business a bit by not doing the traditional wedding day thing, but then I had to follow my heart and do things my way.

Stretching out on the bed against the cool sheets, I sigh with contentment. Jack moves over me and kisses my neck, my collarbones, my breasts. Need grows inside me as I feel his erection pressing against the apex of my thighs. He rests on his elbows and gazes at me and I wriggle so the tip of his cock slips inside me. The anticipation of what's coming sends tingles through my body and I could sing with the joy of it all. If I could sing, that is, because I have the worst voice, as Jack discovered when we finally ventured out for food and ended up at a karaoke bar. Put it this way, we didn't stay long.

'I love you, Mrs Kendrick,' he says.

'I love you too.' Smiling, I stroke my hands over his broad shoulders, caress the tattooed skin I adore. We considered a double-barrelled surname, but I decided I just wanted to take his name to let the whole world know that I am his and he is mine. My wedding and engagement rings glint on my

## Epilogue - Grace

left hand and I admire them, bands of our commitment to each other and the life we're building. 'Now make love to me, husband.'

'I'd better just grab a c—' He makes to move away, but I stop him.

'Don't.'

'What?' His eyes fill with mischief. It's something we've discussed recently but never pinned down. 'You want me to enter you bareback, wife? You naughty little Goldilocks, you.'

He is teasing, but I can see that he likes the idea of being inside me naked. The thought of his skin and my skin together with nothing between us makes my core pulse, so I open my legs wider and run my hands down to grab his ass.

The groan as he enters me arouses me more and soon he's thrusting into me with a force that makes the headboard slam against the wall. I wrap my legs around his waist and he lifts me so he's kneeling and I'm straddling him. We bounce together and he's so deep and big that my core aches, but it's so good and I need him and ...

I shatter into a million fragments as he fills me with his seed.

'That was so fucking good,' he says as he gently moves us around and spoons me in the bed, pulls the sheet over us and kisses my shoulder. 'Do you think we made a baby?'

'I'm not sure, but I think we should get lots of practice in before we go home just to raise the odds.'

'I'm game for that,' he growls.

*Epilogue - Grace*

It's not long before I feel him stirring against me again and as he roams his hands over my breasts, then moves one down and slides his fingers over my already swollen clit, I relax into the knowledge that this is for keeps.

I am his Goldilocks, and he is my Bear.

This is the happy ever after to our own fairy tale.

## *The End*

If you enjoyed *Healing the Billionaire's Heart*, why not read *Meeting the Billionaire Boss* and *Starting Over With the Billionaire* now!

# Also by Wynter Wilde

*Meeting the Billionaire Boss*

**Edward Cavendish:** Losing my wife two years ago was not something anyone expected. Lucille was beautiful and successful, and I thought we'd spend our lives together. Turns out I was wrong. Facing the world feels impossible so I shut myself away in my mansion in the countryside where only my young son can bring a smile to my face.

**Ava Thorne**: I'm broke. More than broke, actually. I have mountains of debt and it's getting worse by the day. I've been working two jobs to support my sick mother and younger brother, but when I'm fired from the one over a mistake that wasn't mine, I don't know where to turn.

**Edward:** My son's nanny is going away on the trip of a lifetime, so I need to find a replacement. It has to be someone we can trust but the thought of having anyone else in my home turns me cold. Plus, there's the inheritance clause that states I must be married on my 35th birthday and the date looms ever closer…

**Ava**: When the opportunity of a lifetime arises in the chance to earn a large sum of money fast, I'm forced to confront my past and decide if I can embrace a future I never dreamt of.

### And it all starts with meeting the billionaire boss…

*Starting Over With the Billionaire*

**Lucas Barrett:** I've a head for business and a body for… well, having a good time. By day, I rule the boardroom. By night, I rule the bedroom. The women I date have no expectations of me and I have none of them. Any hint of one of them wanting more and that's the last they'll see of me.

**Carla Russell:** After over a decade in New York, I've returned to London. It's not what I wanted but sometimes life doesn't work out the way we planned. I fell in love, got married and we talked about starting a family, but tragedy struck and my world fell apart. All I'm certain about now is that I gave my heart once and I know I'll never love again.

**Lucas:** When I bump into a school friend's younger sister at a bar, I consider hitting on her but there's something in her eyes that warns me not to even try. Instead, I find myself offering her a place to stay until she can get back on her feet.

**Carla**: Staying at the luxury city apartment of my older brother's friend was not part of the plan but when I meet him at a bar, I find I'm curious. He was an obnoxious teenager and I used to hate his guts but now he's all grown up and undeniably hot. Plus, it's the coldest winter in years, I have nowhere else to go because the hotels are all full and there's a snowstorm on the way.

***Will Carla find a way to start over with the billionaire or will she leave him behind as the snow begins to melt?***

## About the Author

Wynter Wilde writes passionate and emotional romances featuring brooding heroes and strong heroines.

Connect with her on:

Printed in Great Britain
by Amazon